Geronimo Stilton

TIME WARP

THE SEVENTH JOURNEY THROUGH TIME

Scholastic Inc.

Library of Congress Cataloging-in-Publication Data available

ISBN 978-1-338-58742-5

Text by Geronimo Stilton
Original title *Viaggio nel tempo-7*
Cover by Danilo Barozzi
Illustrations by Silvia Bigolin, Carla De Bernardi, and Alessandro Muscillo
Graphics by Chiara Cebraro and Marta Lorini

Special thanks to Julia Heim
Translated by Beth Dunfey
Interior design by Kay Petronio

10 9 8 7 6 5 4 3 2 1   20 21 22 23 24

Printed in China   62

First edition, February 2020

Geronimo Stilton

THE SEVENTH JOURNEY THROUGH TIME

VOYAGERS ON THE SEVENTH JOURNEY THROUGH TIME

Geronimo Stilton

My name is Stilton, *Geronimo Stilton*. I am the editor-in-chief of *The Rodent's Gazette*, the most famouse newspaper on Mouse Island. I'm about to tell you the story of one of my fabumouse adventures! But first, let me introduce the other mice in this story . . .

Thea Stilton

My sister, Thea, is athletic and brave! She's also a special correspondent for *The Rodent's Gazette*.

TRAP

My cousin Trap is a terrible prankster sometimes! His favorite hobby is playing jokes on me . . . but he's family, and I love him!

Misty Volt

Mistaya is Professor von Volt's niece and a great scholar of ancient history. She always has her head in the clouds and is very focused on her research!

Benjamin

Benjamin is my favorite little nephew. He's a sweet and caring ratlet, and he makes me so proud!

Bugsy Wugsy

Bugsy is Benjamin's best friend. She's a cheerful and very lively rodent — sometimes too lively! But she's like family to us!

Professor Paws von Volt

Professor von Volt is a genius inventor who has dedicated his life to making amazing new discoveries. His latest invention is the Time Tentacle 2000, a new kind of time machine that's causing all sorts of trouble!

UH-OH . . . THE TROUBLE BEGINS!

All my **troubles** began on a Saturday evening. It had been a truly unbearable day. I was finally scampering home after a super-duper long day of work at *The Rodent's Gazette* — and have I mentioned I was working on a Saturday?!

Oh, pardon me, I almost **FORGOT** to introduce myself.

My name is Stilton, Geronimo Stilton, and I run The Rodent's Gazette, the most famouse newspaper on Mouse Island!

As I was saying, it had been a super-duper looonnnng day of work. New Mouse City was voting on new laws to protect the city. Pirate cats were **threatening** Mouse Island, and *The Rodent's Gazette* was helping to find a solution.

By the time I got home, it was already **DARK OUT**, and I was sleepier than the dormouse in *Alice's Adventures in Mousyland*.

Yawning, I tried to put my key in the lock by the light of the streetlamps . . .

And that's how it all started. I didn't n**o**tice there was an enormouse rock on my doormat. What was it doing there? Who knows! I stubbed my **paw** (*yee-ouch!*), lost my balance, and hit my snout against the door to my apartment! **KabanG!**

I began to hop up and down on my good paw,

yowling in pain. I could feel a world record–sized **bump** forming on the top of my snout.

Meanwhile, I tried to think. *Why was there a big rock on my doormat?*

Who could have put it there? And more important, *why?*

Oww, oww, oww, that hurts!

I decided to take a closer look at the rock I'd stubbed my paw on. And that's when I noticed the mysterious rock was wrapped in a piece of paper. So I picked it up and read:

A MYSTERIOUS MESSAGE FOR GERONIMO STILTON!

P.S. READ IT, CHUMP! (BUT DON'T LET ANYONE SEE YOU, OKAY?)

How strange . . . what's up with this paper?

A MYSTERIOUS MESSAGE

Rancid rat hairs, the rock was covered in a very mysterious message!

I picked up the rock, slid it into my pocket, and quickly looked to my right and to my left to see if anyone was watching. Then I scurried inside, locked the door behind me, and, just to be sure, blocked the door with a chair. I lowered the blinds, pulled out the **rock**, and unfolded the paper with the message.

How mysterious ... it was unsigned! Who had sent

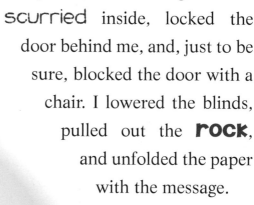

There. Done!

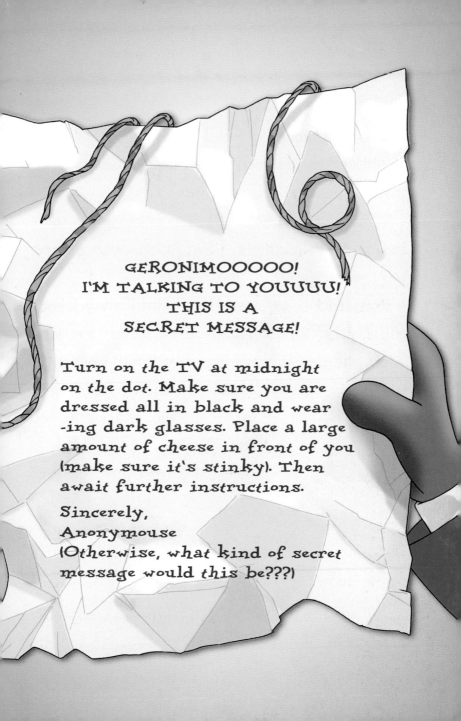

GERONIMOOOOO!
I'M TALKING TO YOUUUU!
THIS IS A
SECRET MESSAGE!

Turn on the TV at midnight on the dot. Make sure you are dressed all in black and wear-ing dark glasses. Place a large amount of cheese in front of you (make sure it's stinky). Then await further instructions.

Sincerely,
Anonymouse
(Otherwise, what kind of secret message would this be???)

this to me, and why? I had no choice: if I wanted to understand, I needed to follow all the strange instructions on the mysterious letter!

I checked my **watch**. There were less than two hours to midnight. I had just enough time to get ready.

First, I looked for the black suit that my friend **Daniel E. Deadfur** had given me for my birthday years before. Now, where on earth had I put it?

I looked everywhere. Finally, I found it

Here is the gift Daniel gave me for my birthday!

It's perfect for your funeral!

Err . . . thanks?

DANIEL E. DEADFUR

A funeral director who always dresses in purple and wears round glasses and a black wig.

on top of a wardrobe . . . or I should say that the suit found me. It fell right on my snout, along with a heavy wooden **trunk**.

I slipped into the black **suit**. It had been chewed by moths and smelled terribly

Heeeelp!

The chest was full of moths!

Ouchie!

of mildew . . . plus it was too tight! Crumbling

Umm . . . cheddar, I had gotten a bit of a **belly** in the last year or two.

I sucked in my breath so the buttons of the jacket wouldn't pop. Then I moved on to the **secret message's** second request: wear dark glasses! I had a pair around somewhere . . . my friend secret agent **OOK** had given them to me.

This time I found them right away: they were in my secret hiding place, along with all my gear for my missions as 00G, which I carry out for **P.S.S.S.T.** (the Powerful Secret Secretest Service Team). I put them on and looked in the mirror.

They made me look so cool and **mysterious**! Still wearing my dark glasses, I left my secret

OOG'S SECRET HIDEOUT

There is a second pair of glasses hidden in this picture. Can you find them?

Lookin' good!

Answer on page 308.

laboratory (I can't tell you where it is, otherwise what kind of a secret would it be?) and scurried back into the house. Then I opened the safe where I kept a wheel of very precious stinky cheese I inherited from my **great-great-great grandfather**.

I put a few **pieces** of cheese on a platter and

Ooops!

Aaack!

I put my paw in a vase of roses . . .

stumbled through the dark — I had turned off the lights and bolted the door and windows — and headed for the living room.

But I forgot to take off those dark **GLASSES**, so I couldn't see a thing! I tripped on the carpet. I tried my best to stay on my feet, but I stuck my paw in a vase of roses covered with thorns, and then I hit my knee against the corner of the table and ended up **SNOUT-DOWN** on the floor. But somehow, I didn't spill a single piece of **cheese**!

MYSTIFYING MYSTERIES!

By now, it was almost midnight. I turned on the TV and sat wearing my dark suit and dark glasses with a bunch of stinky cheese in front of me, just as the secret message had instructed.

Eeeeek!

When it struck midnight, the screen turned **black** . . . and suddenly, I heard a terrifying **HOWL** that froze my whiskers . . .

WOOOOOOO!

A voice as **deep** and *mysterious* as a moonless night announced: "And now, ladies and gentlemice, it's bedtime for all the scaredy mice out there! For we are about to show you . . .

MYSTIFYING MYSTERIES:
IN SEARCH OF
LOST CIVILIZATIONS!"

On the screen, a spotlight illuminated a very familiar snout. I'll give you one guess who it belonged to.

IF YOU'RE NOT ALARMED BY MUMMIES . . . COME ON DOWN!

IF YOU'RE NOT AFRAID OF PHANTOMS . . . COME ON DOWN!

IF YOU DON'T CARE ABOUT CROCODILES . . .

IF YOU DON'T DREAD DISASTERS . . . COME ON DOWN!

IF YOU DON'T PANIC OVER PIRANHAS . . .

COME ON DOWN!

IF TRAPS AND TRICKS MAKE YOU TITTER . . . COME ON DOWN!

IF SPOOKY PRANKS MAKE YOU CACKLE . . . COME ON DOWN!

MOUSE TV

COME ON DOWN, COME WITH MEEEE! OOOOOOH, COME ON DOWWWWWN!

Yep, it was my cousin Trap advertising a show called **MYSTIFYING MYSTERIES**!

Cheese niblets, I had no idea that Trap had started hosting a late-night TELEVISION show! But how was that connected to the mysterious message, the dark suit, the dark glasses, and the cheese?

I didn't understand a thing, so I decided to watch the show even though it wasn't supposed to be for **'fraidy** mice like me!

Trap picked up the microphone. "Mouse friends, welcome to . . . **MYSTIFYING MYSTERIES: IN SEARCH OF LOST CIVILIZATIONS**! In this super-spine-tingling episode, I will reveal the most mysterious mysteries of all time! So hold on to your hats! I'm talking about mysteries like the lost kingdom of **ATLANTIS**! The mystical stone circle **STONEHENGE**! And maybe even . . . a trip into **THE FUTURE**!"

The camera zoomed in close on Trap's snout, and he *winked.* "Not bad, right? These are super-fancy **MYSTERIES**, right? This is not amateur hour! I am a mystery professional, and today I will be helped by my assistant, who will do exactly as I say. Why, this particular mouse doesn't even know who he is yet! Let's all go get him together! Are you ready? Then . . .

"Folloooowwww meeeeeee!"

Now I was really intrigued. I wondered, *Who will this poor* **mouse** *turn out to be?* I felt sorry for the unfortunate rat who would become my cousin's assistant. (*Victim* would probably be a better word for it.) And I felt so lucky it wasn't me this time! You see, I know my cousin Trap well. He really knows how to take advantage of a rodent . . .

Meanwhile, I kept **watching** the TV. Trap was scurrying through the streets of New Mouse City. The camera followed his every move. He turned around and said, "Wait till you see what a SURPRISE this is. I guarantee this cheddarface doesn't suspect a thing!"

Trap leaves the TV studio . . .

He crosses Singing Stone Plaza . . .

I leaped out of my chair. "What a coincidence that's my neighborhood! How odd . . . that's my street! **How peculiar!** This poor rodent lives in my neighborhood!"

Just then my doorbell began to ring.

DING-DONG! DING-DONG! DING-DONG!

He reaches Geronimo's neighborhood . . .

He rings Geronimo's doorbell!

WHO'S THE VICTIM NOW?

I ran to the door and threw it open. Trap stuck his snout in the entryway.

"My dear viewers, here he is!" he **YELLED** at the top of his squeak. "This is the new assistant, secretary, handymouse . . . my cousin Geronimo Stilton!"

Moldy mozzarella, I finally got it: that poor mouse who would be Trap's victim — I mean his assistant — was . . . me! (Of course it was.)

Here he is!

I almost fainted from embarrassment. Trap **DRAGGED** me into my pawchair and thrust a piece of stinky cheese under my snout to keep me awake. Then he stuck a **MICROPHONE** in my snout. "So, Cousin, are you or are you not a journalist?"

"Yes, of course I'm a journalist!"

"And as a **JOURNALIST**, are you ready to face any danger in order to discover the truth?"

"Yes, yes, of course I'm ready for anything . . ." I murmured.

"Did you hear that? Ready for anything! So then you agree to leave with me . . . in search of **MYSTERIES!**"

I shook my snout. "Absolute— " I was about to say, **"Absolutely not!"** but Trap interrupted me.

"You heard that, right, viewers?" he shouted into his microphone. "He said 'absolutely YES'!"

Trap pinched my *tail* and whispered, "Smile, bow, and say 'thank you'! Your public is waiting!"

I no longer had the courage to tell the truth. You see, I'm a terrible 'fraidy mouse, and I *really*

THANK YOU, LADIES AND GENTLEMICE, THANK YOU!

didn't want to go in search of **MYSTERIES**!

As soon as the camera turned off, I began to protest. "Trap, why in the name of cheddar would you storm into *my* house with all those cameras and not even warn me?"

"What do you mean? I did warn you! You found my message, right? You're even dressed in a dark suit and **glasses**!"

"But what was the stinky cheese for?"

"Ah, the stinky cheese. It had three purposes, my dear Geronimo. **FIRST**, it was to help you come to in case you fainted. **SECOND**, it was so I would have something to snack on, because I'm terribly hungry! And **THIRD**, to give me energy — a mouserific adventure is about to begin!

"Move those paws, Cousin; we need to go!" Trap went on. "Remember that now you're my victi — I mean, assistant — and you need to do

Tray of stinky cheese
Yum!
What are you doing?!
Can you find the paper with the mysterious message?

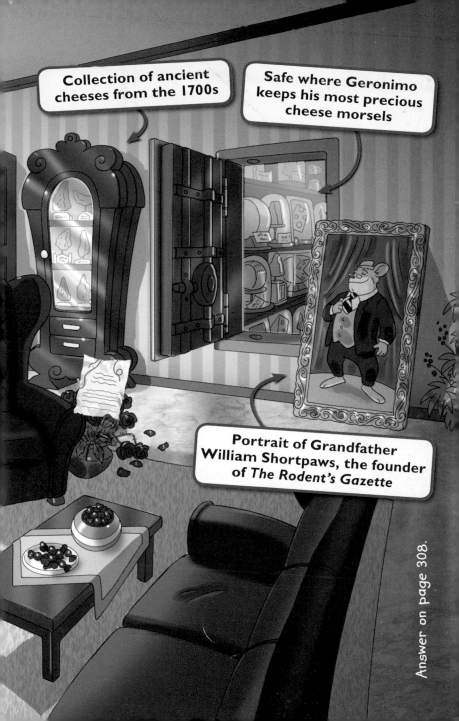

Answer on page 308.

everything I say, including polishing my shoes and washing my dirty socks!"

I complained. "But I don't want to be your assistant! Tomorrow you must explain everything to the public! I don't want to go in search of MYSTERIES!"

Trap lifted an eyebrow. "My audience will be DISAPPOINTED, they will be DISMAYED, why, I think they'll be devastated! Everyone in New Mouse City tuned in and saw you! And you know that my show is the most popular show on Mouse TV, right? No one here in New Mouse City ever misses it."

Just then I heard a ding. My email inbox had begun to fill up with messages. Next, my phone began to ring, and my cell phone began to vibrate . . .

Gobs of Gouda, they were all messages from friends and relatives complimenting me on my COURAGE.

My sister, Thea, called and squeaked, "Well done, Gerry Berry. I had no idea you were so **brave!**"

Next my Aunt Sweetfur called. "My *wonderful* nephew, you were quite **COURAGEOUS**, but won't it be dangerous?"

And Benjamin exclaimed, "Uncle, you've gotten so **TOUGH**! I barely recognize you anymore!"

Then Bruce Hyena called. "Congrats, you cheese ball, you've finally turned into a **REAL MOUSE**! You've made me prouder than a peacock in spring!

Congrats, Uncle!

BENJAMIN

So brave!

THEA

Well done!

HERCULE POIRAT

Is it dangerous?

AUNT SWEETFUR

So great!

PATTY

A real muscle mouse!

I'm proud of you!

MISS RAVEN

BRUCE HYENA

Congratulations!

PATTY

BUGSY

You're so tough, Uncle G!

Just be sure to come back alive, okay?"

Even Daniel E. Deadfur called me. "Well done! You wore my black suit . . . you look just perfect for your **FUNERAL**."

I got a call from every mouse I know. Trap was right — no one misses his show! Even Grandfather William called me. "Well done, Grandson. For once you've done something right!" he barked. "You made the right choice agreeing to go! **MYSTERIES** are very popular with the public. I expect a mouserific **SCOOP** about the most mystifying mysteries in history. Can't wait to see how much our readers like it!"

When I hung up, Trap smirked at me.

"Do you really want to give up, Cuz?" he asked. "Do you really want to look like a scaredy rat on TV? Do you really want to **disappoint** all your friends, Grandfather William, and even Benjamin?"

Alas, my cousin knows me well. I would never disappoint the rodents **dearest** to me in the world, especially not Benjamin.

"No, I don't want to disappoint them," I murmured.

Quicker than a cat with a ball of yarn, Trap pulled out a contract. "Sign here — you're hired! By the way, we leave tomorrow morning at dawn. You have only a few hours left!"

Before I could **read it**, he stuffed the contract into his pocket. I wanted to protest, but then the door to my house burst open and Thea,

Um · · ·

Sign here!

CONTRACT WITH TRAP STILTON

The undersigned, **Geronimo Stilton**, does hereby agree to accept the role of assistant to Trap Stilton for the duration of the program **Mystifying Mysteries: In Search of Lost Civilizations**! He will carry out the roles of:

1) **Following** Trap Stilton on all his secret missions, even to the farthest reaches of time and space
2) **Satisfying** all his desires
3) **Fanning** him if it's hot
4) **Making shade** if it's sunny
5) **Carrying** hot cheese tea if it's cold
6) **Obtaining** cheese snacks during filming, whether Trap is hungry day or night
7) **Telling** jokes to keep Trap happy
8) **Shining** his shoes
9) **Washing** his socks
10) **Doing** everything Trap Stilton demands and more!

10 plus) If I do not obey Trap Stilton's every whim,
       I will be forced to wash his socks (even if
       they're stinky!) for the rest of my life!

SIGNED:

Geronimo Stilton

Benjamin, and Benjamin's best pal, Bugsy Wugsy, scurried in.

They were all dressed in black and wearing **dark glasses** like ours.

Benjamin squeaked for the whole group. "We want to go, too! We want to come . . . in search of **MYSTERIES**!"

I'm the Boss!

Everyone began squeaking at the same time, demanding to know what **MYSTIFYING MYSTERIES** we would uncover.

"I am the boss here, so I decide!" Trap said solemnly. "Here are the mysteries that we will unveil:

> **FIRST:** THE MYSTERY OF ATLANTIS!
> **SECOND: THE MYSTERY OF STONEHENGE!**
> **THIRD:** THE MYSTERIOUS FUTURE!"

"Hooray! When do we leave?" asked Bugsy.

I, on the other paw, **CRIED**, "Umm, one minute! Everyone, stop! How do you think we will uncover

MYSTIFYING MYSTERIES:
In Search of Lost Civilizations!

ATLANTIS!

Did the legendary Atlantis ever really exist? Where is it now? Why did it disappear?

STONEHENGE!

How was it built? How did ancient rodents carry such heavy rocks? And what's the significance of the stone circle?

THE FUTURE!

What is more mysterious than that which hasn't happened yet? What will the future hold?

all these mysteries? Going into the future is impawssible! You would need —"

"A *time machine*!" Trap replied, nodding.

"Exactly, but we *don't* have a time machine, so we can't solve the mysteries," I said with relief. "Great! So no danger, then."

Benjamin pulled at my jacket. "Oh no, Uncle G, that's too bad! I really wanted to go on a journey through time to uncover the most **mysterious** of all **MYSTERIES** in history!"

I patted his head fondly. "It will have to wait for another time, Benjamin. Sooner or later Professor von Volt will invite us to go on another journey through time! Now, to make you feel better, I will get a nice midnight snack, and then we can all go to bed."

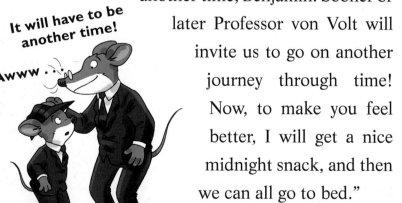

It will have to be another time!

Awww . . .

"I'm down for the snack," Trap said. "But remember that I'm the boss here. So before you do anything else, call Professor von Volt and ask him to lend us a time machine."

"What do you mean? I certainly will not disturb the professor in the middle of the night because of you and your bizarre television show. Plus, I only call him in case of emergencies!"

Trap waved the contract he had just made me sign under my snout. "Better read here, Cuz! Here, use my magnifying glass!"

Smoking Swiss cheese, it said that if I didn't obey my cousin I would have to wash his socks (even if they were stinky) for the rest of my life!

...to keep Trap happy
...his shoes
...shing his socks
...oing everything Trap Stilton demands

...bis) If I do not obey Trap Stilton's every wish, I will be forced to wash his socks (even if they're stinky!) for the rest of my life!

SIGNED:

Geronimo Stilton

Mmm! **Slurp!**

Squeak, Trap had totally trapped me!

I had no choice. I would have to call Professor von Volt. Trap wasn't about to give up. "But before you make that call, come on, make us a snack!" he ordered me. "We are as hungry as tomcats at a mouse buffet!"

I was a bit hungry myself, so I cooked a bunch of spaghetti with melted mozzarella. Then, as everyone was stuffing their snouts, I took the Voltophone and dialed Professor von Volt's secret number.

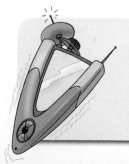

VOLTOPHONE

Professor von Volt's secret locator. Geronimo can use it only in case of emergencies. It has a radar and a satellite navigator.

HOLEY CHEESE, how strange! The professor's phone was busy. But how was that even possible? I was the only one on all of Mouse Island who had his number!

Confused, I hung up. The Voltophone vibrated immediately. *Bzzzz! Bzzzz! Bzzzz!*

The professor was calling me; that's why his **PHONE** was busy! Von Volt's voice quivered with emotion. "Dear Geronimo, come at once, and bring your friends! I will wait for you on the beach at Bimini tomorrow at midnight." *CLICK!*

PAWS VON VOLT

The most famous scientist and inventor on Mouse Island. He works on scientific experiments of all kinds, but his most mouserific inventions by far are his time machines.

DOES ANYONE KNOW WHERE THAT IS?

I returned to the others with my whiskers **trembling**. "Do you want to hear something rattastic? Professor von Volt was calling me the very same *moment* I was trying to call him! He wants us to meet him tomorrow at midnight on the **beach** in Bimini. Does anyone know where that is?"

Benjamin looked at his iRat, a super-modern tablet that's always connected to the internet. He slid it in front of my snout. "Squeak, Bimini is so far away! It's way over in the **BAHAMAS**!"

Umm · · ·

Look here, Uncle G!

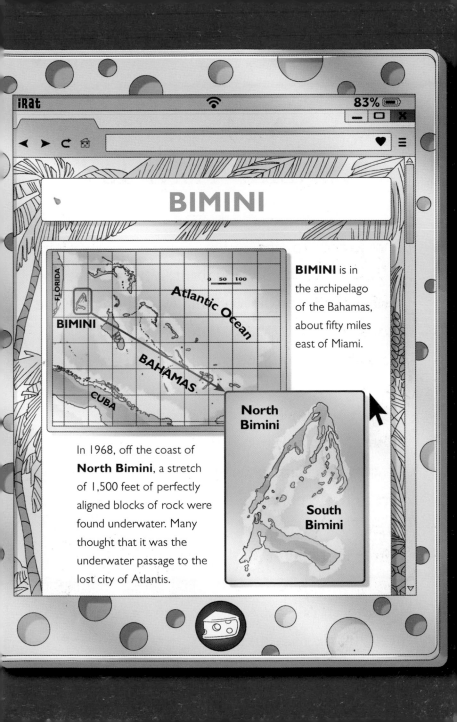

BIMINI

BIMINI is in the archipelago of the Bahamas, about fifty miles east of Miami.

In 1968, off the coast of **North Bimini**, a stretch of 1,500 feet of perfectly aligned blocks of rock were found underwater. Many thought that it was the underwater passage to the lost city of Atlantis.

I was super worried . . .

How could we **reach** the professor in such a short time?

"Did the professor say why he was **calling**?" Thea asked.

"No, he just told me to bring you with me and he urged us to be punctual! He will be waiting for us tomorrow at **midnight** on the dot."

I paused. "I think he wants us to go on another journey through time. So Trap can put this whole idea about the search for mysteries out of his snout. It's waaay toooo dangerous! A *journey through time* like the ones we're used to is better, and those are dangerous enough without any mysteries to solve!"

Trap frowned. "Hmpf! I want to go in search of **MYSTERIES**! And you, Geronimo, remember that you're my vict — I mean, my assistant! You need to help me convince the professor."

I put my paw down. "**No!** I will not help you. I will go only where Professor von Volt says! Traveling through time is no joke. There needs to be a good reason for going."

Trap smiled under his whiskers. "I get it. I'll be the one to convince the professor . . . and I already know how to do it!"

He showed me a mysterious metal briefcase and tapped it proudly. "The **ANSWER** to every problem is in here!"

I cut him off. "I don't care what's in there. I will go only where the professor says!"

Huh?

The answer to every problem is in here!

Everyone else agreed — that is, everyone but Bugsy, who shouted, "Uncle G, you're always so boring! I want to go in search of **MYSTERIES**!!!"

Trap snickered. "Don't worry, Bugsy. Uncle Trap will take you in search of **MYSTERIES**!" Then they began to whisper under their whiskers.

Who knows what those two were plotting? But we had a more urgent matter: how to get to Bimini in less than twenty-four hours! *It was an impawssible endeavor!*

Pssst, pssst, psssst!

Psssst, pssst, pssst!

What are they saying?

I turned to my sister. "Thea, any ideas on how we can get there in time?"

She smiled like a cat who'd swallowed a mouse. "Let me make a couple of calls . . ."

Two phone calls and two hours later, my sister got off her cell phone.

Then she announced, "A dear friend will lend us his sports **car** . . . and another dear friend will take us with his private *SUPERJET* . . ."

Snore . . .

Ugh, so boring . . .

Mouserific! Thanks!

Oh, did I forget to mention? My sister, Thea, has lots of friends who **admire** her and are ready to help her at any hour of the day or night.

A few minutes later, we were in Thea's friend's sports car. He was a **FASCINATING** rodent with a passion for race cars.

I could tell at once that he admired Thea very much.

SPORTS CAR of Thea's first dear friend

PRIVATE SUPERJET of Thea's second dear friend

An hour later, we boarded the supersonic superjet of Thea's other **friend**. He was an actor — and I could tell right away why Thea was friends with him. He was very nice! Unfortunately, both friends were obsessed with *SPEED*!

A third friend let us use his super-speedy motorboat to zoom all the way to the beach in Bimini!

RACING MOTORBOAT of
Thea's third dear friend

LOOKS LIKE REAL FEAR TO ME!

I was so exhausted from the trip, I flopped onto the sand like a jellyfish. The beach was deserted. The moon was full and as **round** as a wheel of cheese, and it was making silvery shimmers on the sea.

As I was **DReamiLy** looking at the sky, a strange thing happened. The waves began to crash against the shore, and I caught sight of movement below. The most **TERRIFYING** creature I had ever seen emerged from the water!

"Heeeeeelp, it's the monster of the seven seas!" I cried, running faster than the mouse who went up the clock.

The **MONSTER** began to call my name: "Geronimooooo, come back here!"

The monster of
the seven seas!
Help!

Now I was even more terrified. "Heeeelp! The monster of the seven seas knows *my name!*"

But a moment later, I realized I'd know that squeak anywhere: it was Professor von Volt! I hurried back to the shoreline, trying to play it cool. "Heh, heh, heh . . . I was just pretending to be scared. I wasn't really scared!"

Bugsy snickered. "Um, that looked like real fear to me! Your whiskers are still shaking." She shook her snout pityingly. "You really are a scaredy-mouse, Uncle G."

But Thea smiled. "That was some SPRINT, Geronimo! You should join the track team."

Umm, actually · · ·

What a scaredy-mouse!

Benjamin just smiled and took my paw. He really is the sweetest!

A porthole in the giant sea monster

popped open, and Professor von Volt appeared. He pulled out a megaphone. "I didn't mean to scare you! This is the **Mega Octo-Portal**, my new secret laboratory. **Please come in!**"

Geronimo!

Answer on page 308.

Inside the **Octo-Portal**, the professor greeted us warmly. "Hello friends, make yourselves at home!" Then he turned to me and asked curiously, "Geronimo, why are you dressed all in black? Are you all going to a **funeral**?"

My ears drooped in embarrassment. "Umm . . . no, no! They are dressed this way because they're fans of Trap's new TV show, *Mystifying Mysteries:*

Yum, yum, yum!

Whisker-licking good!

Yum!

Help yourselves!

Thanks!

Oops!

*In Search of Lost Civilizations.
I,* on the other paw, have been  **tricked** into wearing this ridicumouse outfit!"

"Ah, Geronimo, your clothes are so **elegant** . . . They're giving me inspiration for your trip! But now come, I made you a little **snack**."

The professor had prepared a mouserific meal

Oops . . .

1
The mysterious rodent tripped on a chair . . .

Whoops!

2
And flew into the air, snout over tail! She was about to end up in the cheesecake . . .

There. Done!

3
But I caught her just in time . . .

with **DOZENS OF** cheesy chews and other snacks . . . **yummm!**

Just when I was about to bite into a tasty little cheese puff, a rodent I didn't know scurried in. She had dark fur tied back in a ponytail. She was walking while reading and not looking where she was going. I had just noticed that she wore glasses, **LIKE ME**, when she tripped over a chair! (1)

She ended with her paws up, flying through the air, but a moment before she fell snout-first into the cheesecake (2), I caught her (3)! But I lost my balance (4) . . . and I was the one who ended up with his snout buried in cake (5)! Squeak, I was covered in whipped cream up to my ears. I turned bright red with embarrassment (6)! What a terrible first impression! I looked just like a berry-and-cheese tart! Luckily, the mysterious rodent kept reading and didn't notice a thing . . .

Help · · ·

4

But I lost my balance . . .

Squeeeak!

5

And ended snout-first in the cake . . .

Heh, heh · · ·

6

What a bad impression!

A Peace Mission!

Professor von Volt **scurried** over and introduced us. "Geronimo, this is my beloved niece, **Misty.** She will travel through time with you! Misty, this is my **dear friend** Geronimo."

Misty finally looked up from her book and smiled. "Ah, so you're the famouse Geronimo!" She grabbed my paw and **squeezed** it so hard she nearly crushed it!

"N-n-nice to meet you," I stammered. "What a strong grip you have, Misty! Do you play sports?"

"Yes, a little, just to stay in shape," she replied.

The professor cleared his throat. "Now let me tell you why I asked you to come here. As you know, pirate cats are **THREATENING** Mouse Island.

"I believe we should come to an agreement and avoid a standoff. After all, **peace** is the most

MISTAYA VON VOLT,
known as Misty

PROFESSION: A researcher of ancient history, she teaches at the prestigious New Mouse City University.

She graduated with a degree in comparative mousic archaeology and ancient, medieval, and modern history of ratness. Misty specialized in history of mousic and extra-mousic art. To confirm her theories, she often goes on adventures (and she frequently gets in trouble)!

HER PASSION: Reading. She reads always, everywhere, especially when she shouldn't. She loves Geronimo's books.

HER WEAKNESS: She is easily distracted. Her snout is always in the clouds because she is always brainstorming new ideas for her research.

HER SECRET: She is very athletic and sporty! She would be great in all sports if she wasn't so easily distracted. She never gets discouraged, though, and keeps practicing skiing, figure skating, rock climbing, sailing, judo, and weight lifting.

precious resource! Ancient civilizations have faced many similar problems. That's why I will send you to the **PAST** to learn from their **mistakes** and show all mice that peace is always the best solution! What do you think? Will you help me?"

"**YESSSS!**" we all shouted out together.

Everyone but Trap, who began to grumble,

Well . . .

Yesss!

Yippee!

Hooray!

Great!

I'm sending you to the past!

"The mission sounds fine, but where are we going?"

The professor and **Misty** exchanged knowing looks. "The destination is . . . a mystery!" he replied.

Trap lit up. "A mystery? Okay, then! I don't want to brag, but I am a specialist in **MYSTERIES**! And squeaking of mysteries, Professor, have you seen my new television show?"

But the professor continued: "I will tell you your destination later. But now follow me through the **Mega Octo-Portal** to the secret place where I keep the new **TIME MACHINE**!"

Follow me!

Flying cheese sticks, this was so exciting!

The professor led us up

MEGA OCTO-PORTAL

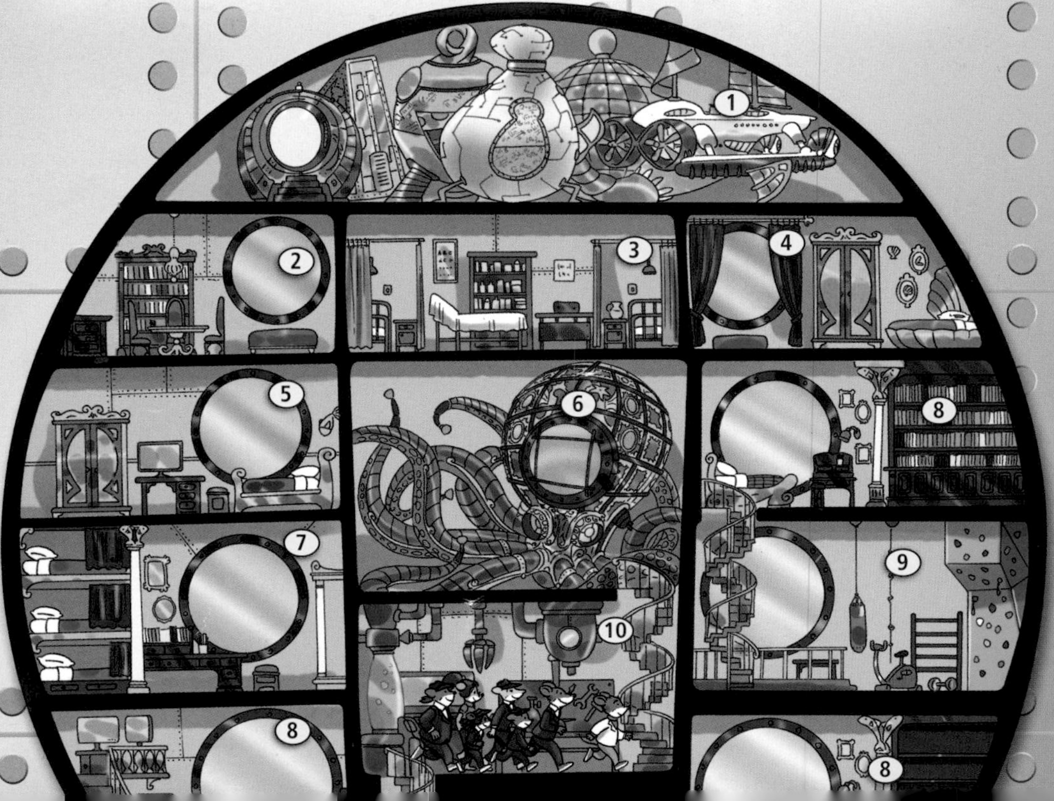

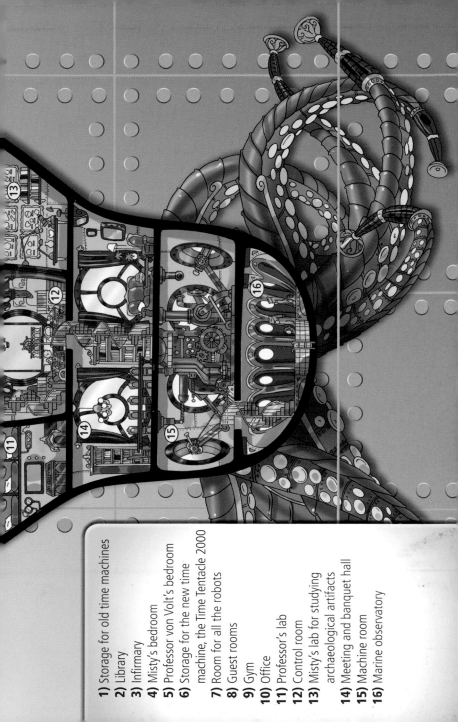

1) Storage for old time machines
2) Library
3) Infirmary
4) Misty's bedroom
5) Professor von Volt's bedroom
6) Storage for the new time machine, the Time Tentacle 2000
7) Room for all the robots
8) Guest rooms
9) Gym
10) Office
11) Professor's lab
12) Control room
13) Misty's lab for studying archaeological artifacts
14) Meeting and banquet hall
15) Machine room
16) Marine observatory

and down the lab until we found ourselves in an enormouse room. In front of us there was a miniature copy of the Octo-Portal!

"Here it is . . . the Time Tentacle 2000!" Von Volt announced proudly. "It is an exact copy of my new secret laboratory, the Mega Octo-Portal, and it can travel through time! It is an extraordinary vehicle. It's amphibious, which means it can travel on land and in water. It can camouflage itself very easily; it can SHRINK DOWN so you can wear it on your finger, just like a ring; it can fly like a helicopter; plus its tentacles contain emergency equipment of all kinds."

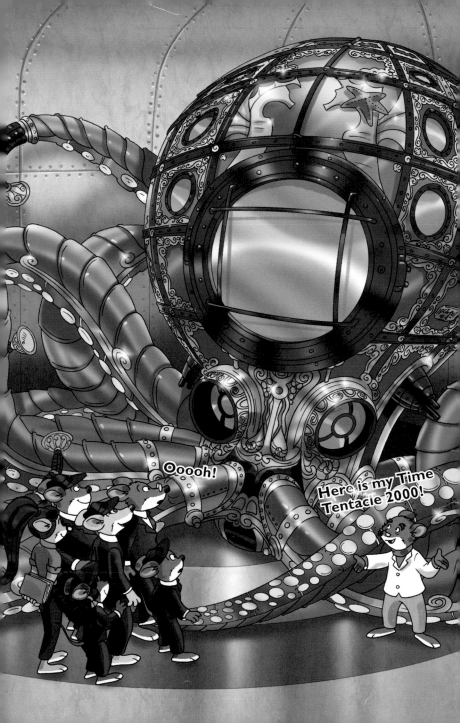

Time Tentacle 2000

NAME: Time Tentacle 2000
SPEED: Ten times faster than the speed of light
PASSENGERS: Holds seven
WEIGHT: Made of weightless electrocheese molecules, so it is very light

The elegant interior of the new time machine

The Time Tentacle 2000 is amphibious, which means it can travel on land and in water.

FLAP FLAP FLAP FLAP FLAP FLAP

It can fly as fast as a helicopter, making its very long tentacles rotate like powerful propellers.

FLAP FLAP FLAP FLAP FLAP!

Trrrrrrrrrrrr!

Its mechanical tentacles can transform in a thousand ways. They can become sharp scissors that can cut through anything, and they can also shoot hail, fog, or a liquid similar to ink!

The Time Tentacle 2000 can shrink down in just a few seconds, becoming a tiny but precious ring.

Seven Travelers for Peace

Cheese niblets, the new time machine was truly **terrific**!

"*Wow*, this is groovier than Gorgonzola!" Benjamin shouted.

Bugsy, who had recently become very interested in fashion, pulled at Professor von Volt's jacket and asked, "Professor, have you already created our uniforms? And the clothes that we'll wear in the different time periods? Huh? Huh? Huh?"

"I already have the special material for your **uniforms** . . . but I didn't know how to design them," the professor responded. "I really like the **dark suits** you are wearing, so I've decided to make the uniforms identical! I'll head to my lab now to work on them; be right back."

He returned a short while later, pushing a clothing rack with our uniforms.

"Here you go! I have equipped them with a new gadget, a **CHRONOTAG**. It's a special microchip that allows your uniforms to transform according to the fashion of the different time periods. I think you'll find these uniforms are just perfect for the seven travelers for peace!"

Here are your uniforms!

"**SEVEN TRAVELERS?** But there are only six of us," Benjamin observed.

"No, here's the seventh," Thea exclaimed. "He was nibbling on my tail!"

Hi, little guy!

Slurp!

Melted mozzarella, the seventh traveler was **Cheezum**! The seventh uniform was for him.

Cheezum jumped around my neck, licking my snout. Slurp, sniff, slap!!

Then an incredible thing happened . . . I knew what he had just said, which was, *Geronimo, I'm so happy to see you!*

"P-P-Professor, Ch-Ch-Cheezum talked inside my he-he-head!" I stammered.

"Hmmm . . . interesting! Cheezum has learned how to communicate with you telepathically, Geronimo. I could explain it better, but there's no time. You need to put on the new uniforms, and I must show you all their **extraordinary** abilities."

We put on the new uniforms. They seemed

*The Cheese-O-Sphere is a time machine Professor von Volt invented for one of our past adventures.

THE SEVEN UNIFORMS

THE UNIFORMS ARE MADE OF AN EXTRAORDINARY MATERIAL PROFESSOR VON VOLT INVENTED FROM THE UNSTABLE MOLECULES OF QUANTICO-CHEESO FOAM. THEY ARE EXTENDABLE, RIP-PROOF, COLLISION-PROOF, FIREPROOF, COLD-PROOF, AND HEAT-PROOF.

SEWN INTO THE INSIDE IS A CHRONOTAG. IT IS A SUPER-POWERFUL MICROCHIP WITH FIVE BUTTONS. WHEN YOU PRESS EACH BUTTON, THE CLOTHING TRANSFORMS TO MATCH THE STYLE OF THE TIME PERIOD. THERE'S ALSO A BUTTON THAT CAN TURN YOU INVISIBLE!

VON VOLT LAB TAILORING
- ANCIENT GREEK MODE
- ATLANTIS MODE
- STONEHENGE MODE
- FUTURE MODE
- INVISIBILITY MODE

identical to the clothes we'd been wearing before, but actually they were very, very different.

"And now let me show you my masterpiece . . . the *TIME GLASSES*!" the professor continued.

"Hey, those look just like my sunglasses!" Trap exclaimed.

"They *seem* identical, but these are no ORDINARY glasses," the professor explained. "They are the latest model of computer. They are unbreakable, indestructible, and adapt to **night vision**. They have a built-in microphone so you can communicate with one another when necessary. Thanks to these glasses and the special panels Misty has created, you'll be able to study up on each time period you visit."

I was about to ask Professor von Volt what our **destination** was when Trap winked and pulled a package out of his **mysterious briefcase**. A delicious smell of almond and vanilla wafted from it . . .

TIME GLASSES

THESE ARE NO ORDINARY GLASSES — THEY CONTAIN THE LATEST MODEL OF MICRO-COMPUTER. THEY ARE UNBREAKABLE, INDESTRUCTIBLE, AND ADAPT TO NIGHT VISION. THEY HAVE A BUILT-IN MICROPHONE FOR COMMUNICATION AND CAN BECOME INVISIBLE.

He pawed the package to the professor and said, "These are for you! They're **cookies** that your grandmother used to bake for you. I asked my

Delicious! favorite bakery — the one that knows all the **recipes** of all the sweets on Mouse Island — to make them for you!"

A *tear* rolled down the professor's snout. "My grandmother taught me to count with these cookies! Ah, just the smell of them reminds me of when I was a wee ratlet . . ."

Trap smirked. "You want these cookies? Then you need to let us travel through time to when I say: to **ATLANTIS**, to **STONEHENGE**, and to New Mouse City of the **FUTURE**!"

The professor smiled under his whiskers. "And so it shall be, Trap!"

Here's the recipe!

Trap pinched my ear. "See, Cuz? I told you I would convince Professor von Volt!"

I was horrified by Trap's behavior. "Shame on you, Trap! Professor von Volt is sending us on a peace MISSION, and all you can think about is your show?!"

But the professor WINKED. "Geronimo, two cookies didn't change my mind, even though they are my favorites! I *want* to send you to Atlantis, Stonehenge, and the future! That's why I came to Bimini. Some writers with a PASSION for archaeology believe they've found the remains of Atlantis here. The ancient philosopher Plato believed that the city of Atlantis was destroyed because of a war that made the gods angry, so

they caused **terrible disasters**. And long ago, there was a war between the Celts and the Romans. I'm sending you to the past to learn how to avoid the same **mistakes**!"

"So why do you need us to go into the future?" I asked.

"Because I'm curious to know how this whole story will end. Will we mice be able to keep the peace on our beautiful Mouse Island?"

Are you ready?

I nodded. "You are wise, my friend." I turned to Trap, Thea, Benjamin, Bugsy, and Misty. "So what are we waiting for? All aboard! Off we go!"

"Hooray for the seven travelers for peace!" Benjamin and Bugsy cried. We scurried into the Time Tentacle 2000.

Another great adventure through time was about to begin...

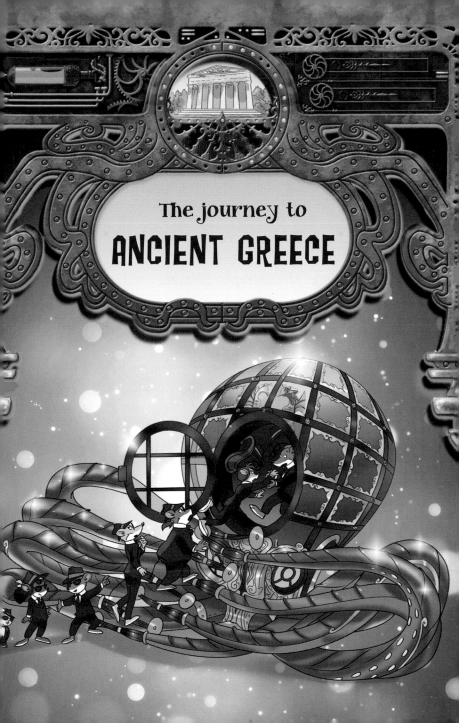

The journey to
ANCIENT GREECE

A CREW OF CHEDDARFACES

We were finally about to leave on another *journey through time*!

Everyone was very serious . . . until Misty tripped over the doorjamb! The book she was reading went twirling through the command center, scattering papers everywhere. I **DARTED AROUND** to gather them, but in my haste I banged my snout against the door! Yeee-ouch!

Oh, I'm so clumsy!

Er, can I help you, Misty?

I wanted to **CRY OUT** in pain, but I didn't want to look like a complete cheesehead, so I pretended it was nothing — even though an **ENORMOUSE** bump was forming on the tip of my snout.

But Trap never lets a chance to embarrass me go by. "Oh, Cuz-undo, you're such a dumbo! You wanted to be kind, but just landed on your behind!" he sang.

"What a crew of cheddarfaces!" Bugsy snickered.

Misty didn't notice a thing. "Oh, cheese, I'm so **clumsy**. My notes! Thank you, Stilton, my dear! I absolutely cannot misplace these notes! They contain essential information for our trip. Now I'll have to figure out what order these belong in."

"Wh-wh-what kind of information?" I **STAMMERED**, alarmed.

START

Answer on page 308.

"Oh, a bit of this and a bit of that," she replied vaguely. "I don't quite remember. But they are very important!"

My whiskers began wavering from the stress. "Quick, we need to find all the notessss!"

Benjamin, Bugsy, and Thea began to hunt all over for the stray *pages* of Misty's notes. Even **Cheezum** tried to help us, but he drooled* all over them!

Meanwhile, Trap **COMPLAINED**. "We don't have time to play treasure hunt with these **notes**! It's time to go in search of mysteries!"

In the end, we found them all. Many of them concerned **ATLANTIS**, the first destination on our trip.

Finally, Thea asked, "So, **Misty**, did you find everything? Can we leave for Atlantis now?"

"**No, not yet!**" Misty squeaked

* Cheezum is made of cheese, so his drool is fondue.

Misty's Notes on Atlantis

The name of the island comes from ATLAS, the son of Poseidon and Cleito, and ruler over the Atlantic Ocean. Atlas was also the first king of the island.

The philosopher PLATO believed that Atlantis was inhabited by people who were half gods, half human, and who conquered many parts of Europe and Africa. After the invasion of Athens failed, Atlantis is said to have sunk into the sea because of a natural disaster.

The GREEK PHILOSOPHER PLATO was the first to speak of Atlantis. According to him, Atlantis was a LEGENDARY ISLAND that was rich and prosperous. He believed it was located beyond the Pillars of Hercules — beyond the borders of the known world at the time.

• Remember to buy two hunks of cheddar and some fresh cream cheese for Uncle Paws!

• Pass to my uncle Paws von Volt to remind him to remind me . . . oh no, I've already forgotten!

• Remember to go to the gym!

BUT DID ATLANTIS REALLY EXIST? Many scholars have asked this question, and there are many THEORIES and books on the subject.

firmly. "First, we need to take a trip to ancient Greece, to the time of Plato. He was the first to speak of Atlantis, so we'll try to meet him. We must ask him for more details to find the legendary land! But before we go, we need to learn how to move, think, and act like **ancient Greeks**."

Trap rolled his eyes. "Let's not waste our time squeaking about ancient Greece! We already know all about it — we've traveled there before."

"Well . . . actually . . . a LITTLE REVIEW might be a good idea," I put in. "Remember, Cousin? The last time we went there, we were all forced to flee Athens with our tails between our paws. It was all your fault!"

Misty looked at Trap over the rim of her glasses. "This time we won't make mistakes. We absolutely *cannot* get into trouble."

"Squeeeeak . . . how in the name of cheddar will we stay out of **trouble**?" I asked anxiously.

OUR TRIP TO ANCIENT GREECE

On a previous journey through time, we'd met **SOCRATES**, the Greek philosopher, who'd invited us to his house and explained his famouse thought: "I know that I know nothing!"

We also attended a banquet at the home of **PERICLES**, the most prominent Athenian statesman of the fifth century BC. While we were there, Trap made more trouble than a rat at a cat convention: he signed me up for a tragedy competition and bet a mountain of money that I'd win!

Finally, after helping Pericles find the **GODDESS ATHENA'S** most precious peplos, we had to run away with our paws up because Trap had, as always, gotten his tail in a twist! He owed a whole pile of money to rodents all over Athens. Holey cheese, what an **ALARMING ADVENTURE** that had turned out to be!

"Something always seems to go wrong when we travel through time!"

"Put on these time glasses. They will help us **immerse** ourselves completely in the time," Misty instructed as she handed us each a pair. She pressed a **button** and a large panel slid out of the command center walls. It showed **Athens** during Plato's time.

I put on the **TIME GLASSES** and was struck squeakless! It really seemed like we were in **ancient Greece** . . .

A FEW SMALL REMINDERS

"**WOW**, these **GLASSES** are cooler than iced cheese!" Benjamin exclaimed.

"They are **marvemouse**!" Bugsy shrieked so loudly, she almost burst my eardrums.

Thea was studying everything carefully. Even Trap was interested. **Cheezum** was licking my snout enthusiastically.

I, on the other paw, was squeakless with awe! Thanks to those amazing glasses, we could see the great philosopher Plato **perfectly**, like he was standing right next to us!

Misty consulted her notes. "Friends, I know you've already been to Athens, but I want to remind you of a few things about ancient Greece.

If we want to meet Plato to ask him for more information about the legendary **ATLANTIS**, we need to make sure we don't get discovered."

She began to search through her notebooks and pulled out a bunch of **PAPERS**, muttering, "I should . . . **UMM** . . . have . . . some . . . **UMM** . . . small reminders . . . that I wrote down . . . but, **UMM** . . . wherever did I put them? I'd lose my snout if it weren't attached!"

Umm . . . where are my notes?

Misty's Notes on Ancient Greece

Between 480 and 323 BC, ATHENS was at the height of its power. This period is known as the classic age of Greek history.

THE CITY OF ATHENS

The highest section of the city of Athens is called the acropolis. The city's most important sacred temples still stand there, among them the PARTHENON. In the center of the lower city is the AGORA, the main square that was also the commercial and economic center for Athenians.

- Remember not to lose these precious notes on ancient Greece!

THE GREEK HOUSE

A very <u>SIMPLE</u> home with rooms distributed around a courtyard. <u>WOMEN</u> and slaves spent most of their time at home. Free men spent their days doing farm work, playing sports, and taking part in public affairs.

FASHION IN ANCIENT GREECE

The clothes in ancient Greece were very simple. Women wore long tunics that were fastened with brooches on their shoulders. During the summer, they left their arms bare. Men wore tunics clasped at the waist with a belt. Young people's tunics were knee-length; older men wore tunics down to their ankles.

SPORTS

All Athenian citizens could participate in athletic competitions that were part of religious celebrations to honor the gods. The Olympics — which are the ancestor of and inspiration for our modern-day Olympic Games — were organized every four years on Olympus.

WOMEN

Unfortunately, in ancient Greece women couldn't take part in public life or politics, participate in banquets, or leave the house alone. They had no assets and were always under the control of their male relatives. They lived in an area of the house that was separate from the men's area, known as gynoecium.

• Go to the library to get a book on acropolises . . . don't forget your library card!

THEATER

The first theatrical performances probably originated from the songs and dances of religious celebrations dedicated to Dionysus, god of wine. The Great Dionysia was a competition that included tragedy and comedy, and all citizens were allowed to participate.

Tragedy competition

As soon as **Misty** mentioned that female rodents couldn't leave their homes alone in ancient Athens, Thea exclaimed, "Great Gouda! That is not going to work for me! How will we move freely around the city?"

Bugsy winked. "Don't worry, Thea; I've got an absomousely brilliant solution: we'll wear men's clothes."

Benjamin high-fived her. "Nice, Bugsy. What a marvemouse idea!"

Bugsy grinned. "It's a bit of a shame, though . . . Women's clothing was so **chic** back then."

"All right, let's hurry up. We need to **leave**, and quick!" I said.

"At last you're squeaking sense!" Trap declared. "Let's goooooo!" He jumped up to the command station and pressed the button labeled **ANCIENT GREEK MODE**. Then he lowered the lever labeled DEPARTURE and the *TIME TENTACLE 2000 DARTED AWAY FASTER THAN THE SPEED OF LIGHT*!

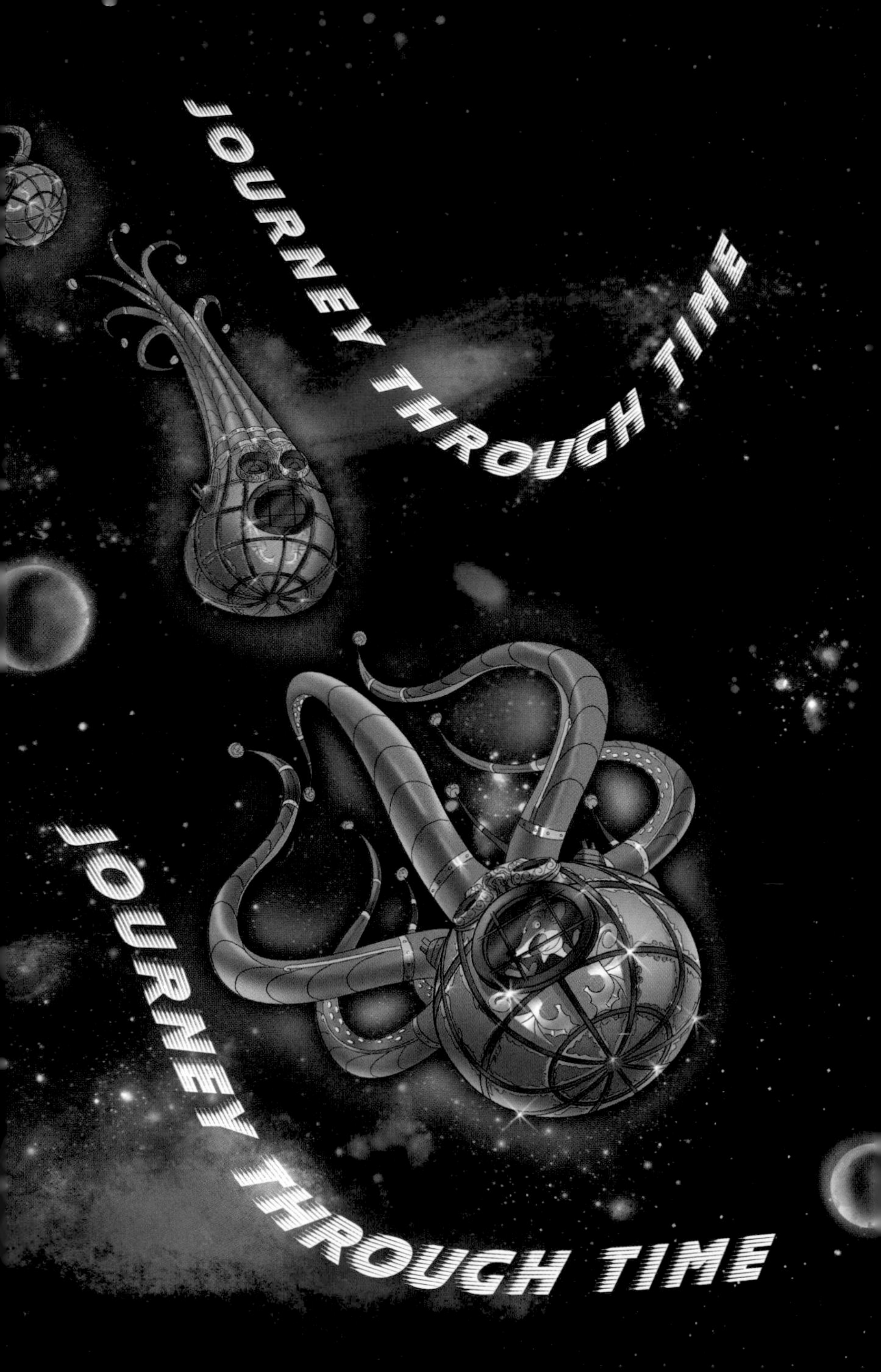
JOURNEY THROUGH TIME
JOURNEY THROUGH TIME

WHERE'D IT GO?

The Time Tentacle 2000 continued bouncing through the various time periods, up and down and up and down!

Meanwhile, my belly was shaking like Brie in a blender. At last, we stopped — thank goodmouse!

We pressed the yellow button on our **CHRONOTAGS** that said ANCIENT GREEK MODE.

Immediately, our uniforms changed into beautiful ancient Greek tunics!

I looked for the lever to shrink the Time Tentacle 2000 and turn it into a ring. Then I noticed a lever with a tag labeled **SHRINK RAY**.

SHRINK RAY LEVER

I pressed it, and a robotic voice rang out: "This is your five-second warning! Scurry away or you'll get **SHRUNK**, too!"

We darted out of the Time Tentacle 2000 as

the robot voice counted down: *"FIVE... FOUR... THREE... TWO... ONE..."*

Fortunately, we made it outside in the blink of a cat's eye. We had arrived in a scenic park in ancient Athens.

But . . . where did the Time Tentacle 2000 — I mean, the ring — end up? My whiskers were quivering with worry . . .

MOLDY BRIE BALLS, WHERE HAD IT GONE?

Squeak! We had to find that ring or we'd be stuck in ancient Athens forever!

Where did the Time Tentacle 2000 go?

Here it is!

After a few minutes of frantic searching, I spotted it. It had **bounced** off behind a column and was rolling away.

I **SPRANG** on it like a hungry cat, but my aim was off, and I ended up smacking my snout on the ground!

Kabonk! Ouchie!

Meanwhile, the Time Tentacle 2000 landed right in some fresh donkey droppings. Ewww, what a terrible stench! And worst of all, I had to put my **PAW** right in the middle to retrieve the ring!

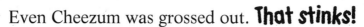

Even Cheezum was grossed out. **That stinks!**

Dear reader, I'll give you one guess who was forced to wear that **super-stinky** ring on his right paw. Yep, it was me, of course.

A pack of flies swarmed around my paw. **What a terrible stench!** But then I noticed a rodent I knew at the other end of the park. It was *him*, really *him* . . . Plato!

We **scampered** over and tried to blend in with the crowd of students around him.

PLATO

Plato's real name was Aristocles, but he was called Plato because of his broad shoulders (from the Greek word *platos*, meaning "broad"). He was a student of Socrates, and he was deeply affected by his teacher's death.

Socrates taught Plato a form of learning through **dialogue**: questions and answers designed to help the student discover the truth step-by-step.

Plato founded a very popular school known as the **Academy**. It was named after the park where it was located, which was dedicated to the Greek hero Academus.

GO, STILTON, GO!

Trap pinched my snout and whispered in my ear, "**Scrape** the cheese out of your ears and listen up, you **CHEDDARFACE**! Check out that rat over there, that gigantic genius — I mean, Plato — he's talking about **ATLANTIS**!"

Crispy cheese chunks, Trap was right! Plato was lecturing about how **POSEIDON**, the god of the sea, had created the island of Atlantis. It was surrounded by two rings of land and three seas that were all *equidistant* . . .

Scrape the cheese out of your ears!

Misty whispered in my other ear, "Did you get that, Stilton? **HOW EXCITING!**" Then she gave me a push. "Go ask him where Atlantis is! **_Go, go, goooooo!_**"

Next thing I knew, I was smack in the middle of the circle of students. They were **glaring** at me and holding their noses.

"How rude! How dare you interrupt our teacher," the first one scolded me.

"Eww! And you're such a stinkrat!" the next one cried.

Plato looked at me intensely, lifting his left eyebrow.

I uttered an apology. "Umm, interrupt the excusation . . . I mean, please excuse the **interruption.**"

Plato lifted his right eyebrow, and I stumbled on, turning redder than a cheese rind with **EMBARRASSMENT**. "Well . . . I . . . I mean . . . ummm . . . I come from **far away**, I've made a very long trip, and . . ."

"It certainly smells that way! When was the last

time you bathed? Last year? You stink, mouse!" the third student exclaimed.

"It's not my fault!" I tried to explain. "There was an ACCIDENT, it's all because of the ring — I mean, the donkey, that is, the donkey's *droppings* . . ."

At that point, the students all burst out laughing. I was making a perfectly awful first impression!!!

I was about to scurry away with my tail between my paws when Plato finally squeaked up. "Stop, everyone, stop! This is the perfect opportunity for me to explain something **important** to you. You need to look beyond appearances. What counts is the substance!

"Look at this rodent. The flies circling around his snout make him *appear* to be a stinkrat! But the substance is that he came from far away to meet me! You can't judge a rodent by his fur. You must learn to disregard appearances."

❓❓❓
WHAT MAKES THIS MOUSE A MOUSE?

Plato continued his lesson, using me as an example. "What makes this mouse a mouse? The tail? The ears? The fur? No! What makes him a mouse is the *idea* that we have of mouse. Thanks to that idea, we see him and we recognize him as a **mouse**! Is that clear?"

THE IDEA OF MOUSE

"Will recognizing him as a mouse get rid of all those flies?" a student snickered under his whiskers.

The lesson went on all afternoon, and my friends and I were **ENCHANTED** listening to the great philosopher. We paid close attention as the students and Plato fired out questions and answers — that was how Plato explained his philosophies.

Chewy cheesecake, it was so exciting!

Benjamin and Bugsy asked a lot of questions, and Plato praised them for their intelligence. Misty took **notes**, and Thea listened intently.

But Trap was impatient. "What a snooze! Tell me something, MR. PHILOSOPHER, when are you going to tell us more about Atlantis? Come on, scurry up! I've got mold growing on my whiskers!"

I thought Plato would get annoyed, but he smiled and answered, "All right, that's enough

HERE'S WHAT PLATO ✻ HAD TO SAY ABOUT THE ✻ MYTHICAL ATLANTIS

👑 Atlantis was a beautiful island located near the PILLARS OF HERCULES in the Atlantic Ocean. The island was divided into ten kingdoms, each governed by a king. These were Poseidon's children, and they believed in respecting the laws that they pledged loyalty to.

👑 The island's CAPITAL stood on a hill surrounded by THREE CANALS OF WATER that alternated with TWO RINGS OF LAND. The rings of land were united by a bridge, and each wall had its own watchtower. The canals were large and easy for ships to navigate — they were used for irrigation and for transporting goods.

♛ The houses of ATLANTIS were simple and built with white, red, and black rocks.

♛ The RICHEST building was the temple dedicated to POSEIDON and CLEITO, which stood in the acropolis, the tallest part of the city: it was decorated with GOLD, IVORY, ORICHALCUM, and SILVER.

♛ The KINGS of Atlantis had to help one another — they couldn't ever be at war. They all needed to AGREE on the empire's military missions. This good and just behavior, however, did not last over the course of time . . .

♛ THE DIVINE RACE OF THE KINGS began to mix with the human race — and then they began to misbehave. Finally, ZEUS decided that it was the proper moment to punish Atlantis.

AND SO, THE ISLAND OF ATLANTIS — IN JUST ONE NIGHT AND ONE DAY — DISAPPEARED INTO THE SEA.

POSEIDON

deep thoughts for today! Now I will tell you a little more about Atlantis . . ."

When Plato finished his story, it was sunset, and the students began RETURNING to their homes. "Unfortunately, no one actually believes in the story of Atlantis," Plato told us with a sigh.

"Master, we believe what you've told us," Misty exclaimed. "But tell us, how can we reach Atlantis? We have come from very far away to find out!"

Plato LOOKED around to make sure no one was listening. Then he replied, "No one knows, because it is a secret, but I have an ancient manuscript with a MAP that shows the way to Atlantis. I also have a mysterious key called the KEY TO ATLANTIS. It will allow you to enter and exit the city alive."

Plato paused for a long time. He stared into our eyes, one by one. At last, he continued, "I can see that you are **trustworthy** mice, so I will show you." He stuck his **paw** under his cloak and pulled out the ancient map and the key to Atlantis.

Misty almost fainted from excitement!

"Master, can you lend us the **MAP** and the **key**?" I asked. "We absolutely must get to

Atlantis: it's the only way to guarantee peace for our people."

Plato was moved. "I will not lend them to you. I will give them to you. I can tell you will make good use of them!"

He looked at me. "Here are my treasures:

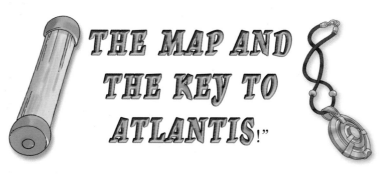

THE MAP AND THE KEY TO ATLANTIS!"

"Thank you, Master," I said seriously. "We will use your gifts to keep the peace on our far-off island! But we must leave at once, for the trip is long and the sun is already SETTING."

We said good-bye, and Plato walked SLOWLY into the hot light of sunset.

When the great philosopher had gone, I pressed

the tiny button on my ring. In a flash, the Time Tentacle 2,000 returned to its normal size. We scurried aboard, ready to face the next stage of our **JOURNEY**: the legendary city of Atlantis!

Then, suddenly, I remembered the tragic end of the legendary island of Atlantis . . .

Squeeeak, how terrifying! Would we be overwhelmed by waves? Crushed by an earthquake? Or struck by a meteorite? We would soon find out . . . unfortunately!

How horribly horrifying!

The journey to
Atlantis

I Want to Gooooo Home!

I thought of the dangers we could face in Atlantis, and a chill went down my tail.

I DIDN'T WANT TO BE OVERWHELMED BY AN UNEXPECTED WAVE, OR CRUSHED BY AN EARTHQUAKE... OR SPLATTERED BY A GIANT METEORITE!

Panic washed over me. I hurled myself across the command panel and cried, "Stop! I don't want to go to Atlantis! I want to go hooooome!"

My friends grabbed me by the tail and tried to drag me away, but I refused to give up.

"It's okay. Calm down, Gerry Berry!" Thea tried to *reassure* me. "There's no need to think that

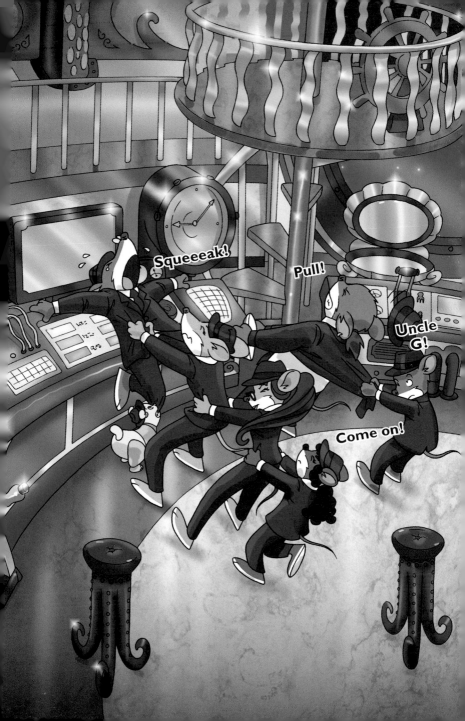

we will get to Atlantis *exactly* at the moment it's going to be **DESTROYED**."

"Yeah, no one knows *exactly* when it was destroyed," Misty added thoughtfully.

"That's *exactly* why I don't want to go! I'm too fond of my fur to put it at risk!" I **YELLED**.

Trap **WAVED** my contract under my nose. "You signed this, so you will do what I say, or you will wash my **socks** (even if they're stinky!) for the rest of your life!"

You will do as I say!

I didn't want to wash Trap's socks (they were *waaaaay* too stinky!), but I couldn't help myself. I was **frozen** by terror, and nothing could make me move.

Then I noticed Benjamin, Bugsy, and Thea were whispering to one another . . . How odd!

Suddenly, Bugsy yelled, "Uncle G, there's a scorpion on your taaaaiiiillll!"

Terrified, I turned to check my tail. All at once, everyone darted toward the **CONTROL PANEL**.

Before I realized what was happening, they'd pressed the button for **ATLANTIS**, lowered the lever that said DEPARTURE, and the Time Tentacle 2000 had darted forward!

Holey cheese, we were moving! Immediately, my sight got blurry, my snout started spinning, and my knees buckled in fright!

"I'm fainting!" I barely managed to squeak.

And then I fainted.

I came to a few moments later to discover my cousin Trap POURING a bucket of water on my snout. "Waaaake up, cheesehead! Does this seem like a good time to pass out? We need to get ready to visit ATLANTIS, THE CITY OF MYSTERIES!"

He started slapping my snout, yelling, "Come on,

I'm fainting . . .

get up! I need you in tip-top shape, **SHARP**, get it? You're my assistant, remember? Now hop to it: You need to take notes, draw sketches, take pictures, and **record** everything we see! Got it? I have a show to do, and you need to **HELP ME**!"

My sister was more sympathetic. "How are you feeling? Sorry, Gerry Berry, but we had to do it: We needed to get you away from there; it was time to go. We did it for your own good, or should I say, for the good of all mousekind. Remember, we're on a peace **MISSION**."

"Snout up, Uncle G," Benjamin tried to comfort me. "Everything will be all right, don't worry!"

"Look sharp, Uncle G! You can do this!" Bugsy shouted in my ears.

Cheezum tried to comfort me, licking my snout and covering me with cheese!

Misty just stared at me in confusion and pinched my tail. "Stilton, my dear, I didn't take you for such a cheese puff!" Then she pulled out her

I didn't take you for such a cheese puff!

NOTES and turned toward the group.

Umm . . .

"We all need to get ready for our visit to **ATLANTIS**, or they will discover who we really are . . . and then we'll truly be in trouble! That would be a complete cat-astrophe! Then

Geronimo would be right to faint!"

She pressed a button on the wall of the **CONTROL PANEL**, and a map showing the city of Atlantis appeared.

Trap pinched my snout and put my *TIME GLASSES* on. "Cousin, open your eyes and get ready to learn . . . or you'll be washing my socks for the rest of your life!"

The others quickly donned their time glasses. We were all breathless before such a **marvel**! It really seemed like we were in Atlantis.

There, done!

BOING! BOING!! BOING!!!

What a gorgeous sight! But as we GAZED at Misty's special effects panel, I realized that I felt terribly Woozy.

The Time Tentacle 2000 (*as usual*) was BOUNCING up and down like a fresh ball of mozzarella.

UGHHHHHH!!

And my stomach was getting shaken and stirred like a Swiss smoothie!

Trap **LOOKED** at my greenish snout and groaned. "For once please try not to make us look softer than a ricotta roll! Pretend you are an **adventurous** and courageous mouse for a change!"

"I'm not doing it on purpose!" I protested. "It's not my fault I suffer from seasickness, carsickness, airsickness, fear of heights . . . not to mention **time sickness**!"

Misty pinched my tail (*again!*). "Stilton, my dear mouse, you need to pay attention, okay? Or you're sure to get in trouble in Atlantis . . . and then you *really* won't feel well!"

She pulled out a stack of paper scraps full of notes on **ATLANTIS** . . .

Misty's Notes on Atlantis

THE NAMES OF THE TEN KINGS

The ten kings of Atlantis, all descended from Poseidon, were: Atlas, Eumelus, Ampheres, Euaimon, Mneseus, Autochthon, Elasippus, Mestor, Azaes, and Diaprepres.

THE CEREMONY OF THE TEN KINGS

Every five or six years, the ten kings of Atlantis united to discuss the interests of the kingdom and to find out if anyone had broken the law. Any lawbreakers would be judged. The assembly met in the temple of Poseidon, where they renewed their allegiance to the laws of the kingdom.

• REMEMBER:
MONDAY
MEETING WITH THE PAPYROLOGIST.

FASHION IN ATLANTIS

No one knows what the fashion was in Atlantis! But we can imagine that it was similar to that of ancient Greece, with soft tunics embroidered with sea-themed designs.

BYSSUS

We can also imagine that their clothing was made of byssus, which is a soft and precious fabric similar to SILK. It's made using the fibers produced by some mollusks. In antiquity, this fabric was used to make clothing for important people.

ORICHALCUM

According to Plato, nature thrived in Atlantis, and the land was rich with precious metals. In particular it was full of orichalcum, a mysterious metal that was as red as fire. This mineral was considered second only to gold.

IMPORTANT:
remember to brush your teeth three times a day!

EVEN MORE IMPORTANT:
don't ever mistake paw cream for toothpaste!

As soon as **Misty** was done explaining, Bugsy exclaimed, "I can't wait to **dress** like they do in Atlantis!"

"Me, too! I'm more curious than a cat about Atlantis couture," Thea squeaked.

"So let's shake a tail! We can transform our uniforms and check it out," Misty said.

And so we all pressed the pink button on our **CHRONOTAGS** labeled ATLANTIS MODE.

VON VOLT LAB TAILORING
- ANCIENT GREEK MODE
- ATLANTIS MODE
- STONEHENGE MODE
- FUTURE MODE!
- INVISIBILITY MODE!

A moment later, our uniforms transformed into elegant Atlantis-style clothes! Misty pulled out a notebook and began to sketch us.

Misty's sketches

Blue clothing

A precious shawl used as a belt!

Flowing fur-dos

Earrings and accessories with sea-themed embroidery

Precious jewelry

Misty showed me her drawings. "What do you think, Stilton?"

But I couldn't respond, I was so terribly time sick! **Glurb!** This ride was bumpier than blue cheese! Luckily, the Time Tentacle 2000 finally stopped. We were in Atlantis at last!

Carefully, I hung the KEY TO ATLANTIS — the mysterious seal that Plato had given us — around my neck and peeked out the window. It was nighttime, and there was no one around — it was the perfect moment to leave the time machine without anyone seeing. Quickly, I pulled the shrink lever. Immediately, the robotic voice began to count down: *"FIVE... FOUR... THREE... TWO..."*

PAWS OFF THE PEARLS!

We dashed out of the Time Tentacle 2000 a second before we got shrunk!

Squeak, we moved fast!

I slipped the time machine — which had transformed into a **ring** — around my finger. We were really in **ATLANTIS**!

The island was surrounded by three concentric rings of **water** and two of land, just as Plato had described. Its buildings were covered in a shiny reddish metal that sparkled in the moonlight.

WHAT A SPECTACULAR SIGHT!!!

How fabumouse!
Squeak!
Marvemouse!
Wow!
Oooh!
Mouserific!
Slurp!

We were standing before the first bridge that linked the five **rings** of land and sea. In front of us was a circular wall covered in engravings and an ornate orichalcum gate, decorated with enormouse sparkly **PEARLS**.

I noticed that there was no guard at the gate . . . *weird*!

Trap stroked his whiskers thoughtfully. "Hmm, my paws are itching to put two or three of these pearls in my pocket. There are so many, no one will notice a few are missing. And I'd be **RICH**, so **RICH**!"

I will become so rich!

Get your paws off those pearls!

Trap said. I could tell he was up to no good, just from the look on his snout.

"Shame on you, Trap!" Thea scolded him. "We are in ATLANTIS on a peace mission, and all you can think about is MONEY!"

I pulled him by the tail. "You pest, get your paws off those pearls!"

Trap brushed our **worries** aside. "Geronimo, I order you to help me! Otherwise you'll be washing my socks (even the stinky ones) for the rest of your life."

Shame on you, Trap!

I had to put my paw down. "I would rather wash your stinky socks for the rest of my days than steal from this **BeaUTiFUL** piece of art!"

I began to pace **BACK** and *forth* like a cat outside a mousehole, wondering how to open the gate. There was no lock, and I didn't see a handle anywhere.

Before I could get a better look at the **door**, it burst open. I leaped back, crying, "Cheese niblets, did this gate read my mind?" Only then did I notice that Plato's seal had **lit up**.

The seal lit up!

A ray of light shot from the center of the seal right at the gate! The seal really was **the key** to enter the mysterious city of Atlantis!

With our tails ᵗʳᵉᵐᵇˡⁱⁿᵍ, we scurried through the gate to the city. It ᵣₑₐₗₗᵧ seemed like a dream, so to be ᵛᵉʳʸ sure that I

Squeak! wouldn't faint, I pulled out one of my whiskers. Squeak, that hurt!

Yep, it was true. I was **truly** awake, super-duper awake!

We used the **KEY** to pass through another wall and cross more bridges and get through more gates. We **WALKED** for hours and hours . . . and hours and hours . . . and hours and hours . . . and hours and hours . . . and hours and hours . . . and hours and hours . . . and hours and hours . . .

Soon, the sun **CAME UP**, and we reached the last gate and the last circular wall. But it was locked. I noticed that it was covered in the same metal as the seal around my neck — **orichalcum**! There we ran into a squad of guards armed with lances.

"We're in big trouble now," I muttered.

"These rats will turn us into **mousemeat**!" I was about to faint from fright, but luckily the guards smiled and called out: "**WELCOME TO ATLANTIS!** The queen awaits you."

Welcome!

WELCOME TO THE PALACE!

As we followed the guards, I cleared my throat and asked, "The queen is waiting? I mean . . . she already knew we were coming?"

The guard raised a confused EYEBROW. "Of course she knew of your arrival! You have the map, the KEY TO ATLANTIS, and you are dressed so elegantly . . . so you must be important rodents invited to the ceremony of the ten kings. But you are early. The queen was expecting you tomorrow, along with the other guests."

I was about to tell him that he was mistaken. "I hope Her Majesty will excuse us, there has been a terr —" I began.

I wanted to add "a terrible mistake," but Thea stepped on my tail, whispering, "Gerry Berry, I'm warning you . . . don't make us look **soft** as cream cheese!"

We're early!

Misty covered my snout with her paw. "There has been . . . really incredible weather: calm **SEAS** and favorable **WINDS**," she declared. "So we arrived ahead of schedule. I hope Her Majesty will forgive us."

The guard smiled. "The **QUEEN** will be happy to host you an extra day, even if she has unfortunately not been in good health lately . . ."

Meanwhile, Misty whispered, "Stilton, dear mouse, we need to pretend we've been invited for the **ceremony of the ten kings**! Remember what I told you about the ceremony? I'm warning you, don't make us look **soft** as Swiss cheese!"

I tried to remember, but . . . nothing came to mind. "Umm, yes, of course, that ceremony . . . the **super-famouse** one where there were, umm, you know . . . the ten kings and . . ."

Misty twisted her **whiskers**. "Stilton, my darling cheese puff, I expect better from you! You need to concentrate, you need to pay attention, and you need to use your neurons!"

Squeak, what a bad impression I'd made!

And then Trap had to go and make it worse. "I always tell this **cheesehead** that he doesn't work hard enough!

I expect better from you!

Umm . . .

What a cheesehead!

"By the way, Cuz — I mean, *assistant*, are you taking notes?" He stuffed an enormouse **notepad** and pencil in my paw. "Come on, Cuz — I mean, assistant! You better get busy if you don't want to wash my **SOCKS** for the rest of your life!"

I began to look around, carefully observing the city and jotting down everything **interesting** I saw.

Bugsy and Benjamin, who were super enthusiastic, pointed out this and that. "Uncle G, did you notice the **GARDENS**?"

"Uncle G, look what splendid clothing that ratlet is wearing! It's decorated with sapphires!"

"And that palace **DOWN THERE**, did you see how it sparkles in the sun? I'll bet it's made of gold . . ."

A guard exclaimed proudly, "That is the royal palace. It is covered in ORICHALCUM. THAT IS WHERE OUR BELOVED QUEEN LIVES . . ."

Cheezum trotted next to me and wagged

his tail eagerly. He had a whole bunch of new information to feed on! He was so excited, he leaped up and licked my snout, covering my whiskers with melted cheese.

Lick . . . Grunt . . . Slurp!

(What a beautiful place! Why don't we move here, too, mouse?)

I replied in my mind: *Because we are on a mission to* **defend** *peace on Mouse Island! Remember?*

He licked my face once more. All he said in response was:

Lick . . . Grunt . . . Slurp!

(You're right!)

The head guard whispered in my ear, "I shouldn't tell you this, but I LIKE you, so I will warn you . . . be careful! Don't trust anyone. There are many dangers here. Remember, all is not what it seems."

I wanted to ask him more, but he had already

ordered the guards, "About snout!"

With that, they marched off. My whiskers were trembling with terror. I called after him, "Wait, what do you mean? What's not as it seems?"

But a paw covered my mouth, and a threatening squeak thundered, "It means don't stick your snout in things that don't concern you, Stranger!" Then he added, "Welcome to the palace!"

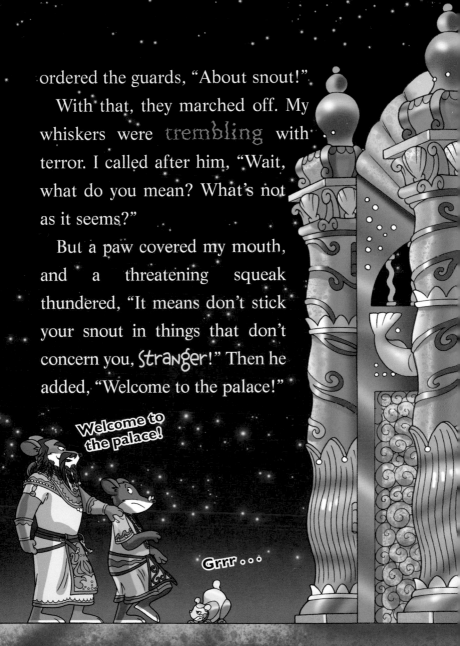

Welcome to the palace!

Grrr...

THE ROYAL PALACE OF ATLANTIS

This reconstruction is imaginary; there is no archaeological evidence of the existence of Atlantis.

THE ROOMS OF THE PALACE
1) The throne room
2) The queen's room
3) The king's room
4) The heirs' room
5) Triton's room (the banquet hall)
6) The seahorse room
7) The pearl room (the music room)
8) The octopus room (the queen's study)
9) The dream weavers' room
   (the guests' room)
10) The jellyfish room
11) The royal basement

DON'T LIKE
THAT RAT!

The threatening squeak belonged to a rat who was as massive as a muskrat, with dark, penetrating eyes and whiskers pointing downward. He was wearing a long tunic and had a big ring of keys attached to his belt. His fur was in a ponytail, and his beard was split into many braids.

He introduced himself. "I am Aristomous Boltbar, the key master. I guard the secret of the keys of Atlantis and control who enters and exits

ARISTOMOUS BOLTBAR

The key master is the keeper of the secret of the keys to Atlantis. He controls who enters and who exits the city, and he holds the secret maps to the royal palace. He belongs to an ancient dynasty of key masters. He would like to marry the daughter of the queen and become king.

the palace. I also make sure that quacks and con artists don't get in! Nothing gets past me . . ."

Cheezum growled at him. Grrr . . . grrr . . . grrr! *(I don't like that rat at all, Geronimo!)*

I pet him to calm him down, thinking: *Be good, little guy, or we'll end up in* trouble*!* Then I replied. "I . . . ummm . . . I'm Geronimos Stiltonides, and these are Mistydora, Trapolos, Theodora, Benjaminos, and Bugsora. We are ambassadors from faraway New Mouse Citoide."

Aristomous interrupted me suspiciously. "New Mouse Citoide? I don't know it. It must be **VERY** far from the Pillars of Hercules!"

I was about to say, "Huh? The Pillars of who?" but luckily

THE PILLARS OF HERCULES

In antiquity, the Pillars of Hercules marked the extreme end of the known world. Geographically, they corresponded to the Rock of Gibraltar and Jebel Musa.

Misty squeaked for me. "Of course, our island is **very, very, very** far from the Pillars of Hercules. We have made a very long trip to get here!"

As we squeaked, the **key master** led us through rooms and halls, and staircases and bigger staircases, and little rooms and big rooms, and banquet halls and dancing halls, until we reached a door that was entirely covered in orichalcum and decorated with marvemouse bas-reliefs of strange-looking sea creatures.

Aristomous knocked, and then he flung open the door and announced, "Your Majesty, here are the ambassadors who have arrived from far-off New Mouse Citoide!"

We entered and bowed before a tall throne where a very beautiful, very pale female rodent was seated. It was Her Majesty Atlaya, the queen of Atlantis! Next to her there were two

little ratlets who were about Benjamin's and Bugsy's age and looked very sweet: the prince and princess of Atlantis.

We knelt before the queen, but **Cheezum** immediately ran to the two little mouselings, wagging his tail. Then he jumped up to the princess's neck and licked her snout.

Lick! Slurp! Grunt! *(What nice snouts you have. I hope we become friends!)*

I tried to stop him, thinking, *Cheezum, come back here! Don't be rude!* But the two young rodents didn't seem offended — in fact, quite the opposite!

They immediately began to play with Cheezum. "Your little GUY is so sweet!"

"His name is Cheezumide," Benjamin said. "I, umm . . . I'm Benjaminos, and she is Bugsora. What are your names?"

Your Majesty . . .

"My name is Delphine, and this is my brother Delphone. Do you want to play?"

The young rodents had already become friends!

The queen smiled. "Thank you for bringing a little happiness here." Then she noticed the key around my neck. "I see that you possess the key to Atlantis, but I don't remember **MEETING** you."

Thea was quick to respond. "We have never been here before. Our ancestors hid the key to Atlantis and we have just found it."

"Then **WELCOME TO ATLANTIS**!" the queen exclaimed. She clapped her paws and ordered her staff, "Make sure that the best accommodations are prepared for the ambassadors of New Mouse Citoide, who have finally returned to **ATLANTIS**! And tonight we will prepare a banquet in their honor, with music and dancing."

Then she turned to us and said with a sigh, "If you'll excuse me, I'm a bit tired . . . I will expect you at sunset in Triton's room for the banquet."

We bowed to the queen and followed her servants outside the throne room.

"Uncle G, can we go play with our new friends?" Bugsy squeaked.

"Of course, but get back here in time for the banquet," I said.

So Benjamin and Bugsy *ran* off with Delphone and Delphine, along with Cheezum, who was wagging his tail happily. **Grunt! Sgrrf. Slurp! Lick!** (*Good-bye, Geronimo! Finally, there'll be some fun!*)

As soon as we left the throne room, we found the **key master**, who hissed in my ear, "Rat, I saw that *she* took a liking to you . . . **be careful**! Keep away from her, or you'll regret it!"

Keep away from her!

Umm · · ·

OPEN UP,
CHEESE PUFF!

SQUEAK, HOW SCARY! My fur turned as pale as a ball of mozzarella.

My sister noticed right away. "What happened? Gerry Berry, you're **paler** than a ghost, you're **shaking** more than a mouse at the North Pole, and you're —"

"You're more terrified than a **tarantula**!" Trap interrupted.

"Th-that m-mouse gives me ch-ch-chills!!" I stammered. "I think something mysterious is going on here. Remember how the head guard warned us? Come to my room later, and we can discuss it privately."

"Hooray! At last we are going in search of **MYSTERIES**," Trap rejoiced.

"We need a code word," Misty suggested.

Trap snickered. "I've got one: **Open up, cheese puff**. And Geronimo has to respond, 'Your wish is my command!'"

I tried protesting, but it was no use: everyone thought it was a great idea.

The servants led us through marvemouse hallways full of marble statues and mosaics in all the shades of the **deep blue sea**. Then we went up a magnificent crystal staircase and crossed enormouse rooms with mirrors and bas-reliefs made of **orichalcum**. It seemed like we were walking for hours! We walked so far that smoke started coming out of my paws! The royal palace was enormouse.

Just when I couldn't take another step, the servants announced, "Here are your rooms."

I was struck squeakless. The walls were covered in BLUE CRYSTAL and orichalcum! I was so tired, I plopped down on the big canopy bed, but immediately there was a knock on the door.

"Code, please!" I said, hurrying to open it.

From the other side I heard, "**Open up, cheese puff!**"

"Your wish is my **COMMAND**," I muttered huffily, turning the knob. "Why are you bothering me now?"

Open up, cheese puff!

Your wish is my command!

"Because you are here to do what I say!" Trap replied. Thea and Misty walked in behind him.

"I **AM NOT**! Even though, every once in a while . . . at times . . . now and again . . . occasionally . . . every so often . . . I let you boss me around, I can make my own choices!" I said hastily. "But let's cut to the cheese. We have more important things to worry about. Why did the key master threaten us? WHY??"

"I don't know; it's a mystery." Misty sighed.

"A mysterrrryyyy?!" Trap exclaimed. "I'll handle this! I'm an expert in mysteries!"

Thea rolled her eyes. "The point is: Why does Aristomous want us to stay away from the queen? WHY??"

"It's strange, very strange . . ." I said thoughtfully.

I began to think . . . and think . . . and think . . . and think and think and think and think and think and think and think and think and think and think and think and think and think and think and think . . . until SMOKE came out of my ears!

At last, I exclaimed, "There's only one way to find out. We need to stay close to the queen."

Thea had been thinking, too. "Mouse friends, the time has come to try . . . invisibility mode!"

Umm . . .

Ummmm . . .

Let's see . . .

Ack!

"Great idea!" I exclaimed. "We can use it to stay near the queen and find out more about the key master without anyone **SEEING** us."

We pressed the blue bottom on our chronotags and immediately turned invisible! Then we **HEADED** toward the queen's quarters.

THE PRESSURE, THE ANXIETY, THE STRESS!

Being invisible was very stressful! FiRST OF ALL: Invisibility mode made the uniforms overheat, and my whiskers began to drip with sweat! **Oh, the pressure!**

SeCoNDLY: Every time we passed someone, I was afraid they would see us! **Oh, the anxiety!**

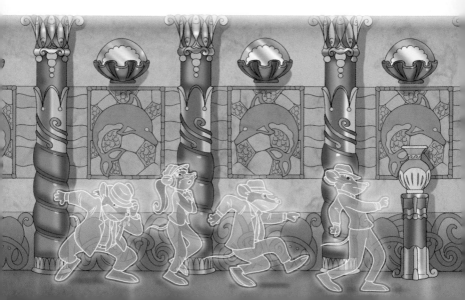

THIRDLY: We had to be silent. No one could see us, but they could hear us! Oh, the stress!

Staying silent might not sound that hard, especially for a mouse, but I have been known to trip over my own paws. Not to mention **Misty**, who was a real champ at stumbling when she was distracted! At least three times, I grabbed her paw just in time to stop her from knocking over a vase. Squeak! Oh, the pressure! Oh, the anxiety! Oh, the stress!

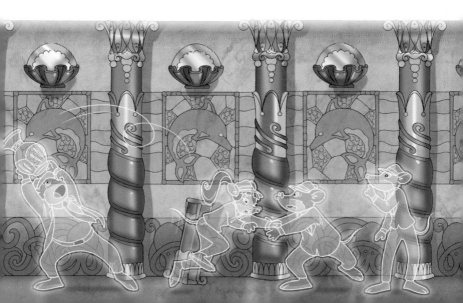

At last, we managed to **enter** the queen's quarters, following on the paws of a group of ladies' maids.

We did it! I thought in **RELIEF.** *Everything went ok* — And that's when the last maid, who hadn't SEEN me (obviously, I was invisible!) slammed the door on my snout. Oh, the pain!

Oh, the pressure! Oh, the anxiety! Oh, the stress!

I was about to cry out in pain, but luckily Thea

Hee, hee . . .   Shhh . . .   Ouchie!

The queen's medicine!

clapped a paw over my snout.

At that moment, Aristomous, the **key master**, knocked on the door!

Aristomous approached the queen's couch and bowed with respect. Then he said **sweetly**, "My queen, you seem better today! I came to make sure you're taking your **meDiCine** . . . it has done you much good!"

The queen gestured that she was getting up. "My dear **ARISTOMOUS**, thank you for your

devotion! You have been so kind to get this medicine for me from so far away. But it's so bitter . . ."

But one of her maids insisted, passing her the goblet with the medicine. "Your Majesty, I know that it tastes bad, but it will cure you. Come now, drink up! It's for your own good."

The queen sighed. She pinched her nose and swallowed the medicine. "Let's hope it works

quickly. I'm feeling WEAKER and WEAKER," she *muttered*.

"It takes time, Your Majesty. Now rest. You need to be in shape for the banquet tonight," Aristomous said. Then, with a small bow, he left.

As he passed by us, I thought I noticed a sinister smile on the key master's face. How strange! So I whispered to the others, "Pssst, quick, let's follow him!"

We darted out after him and managed to leave a moment before the door closed behind us. But when we reached the hallway, the key master had disappeared. How strange! Where had he gone?

We realized that we, too, needed to prepare for the banquet, so we scurried back to our rooms. Once we'd reached them safely, we pressed the pink button on our **CHRONOTAGS** and were immediately dressed in Atlantis fashion again.

Suddenly, the door burst open. It was Benjamin and Bugsy, and they were super excited. "Uncle G, this palace is full of secret passages!" Bugsy cried.

Benjamin handed me a map. "Look, Uncle, this is the map of the secret passages! Delphine and Delphone gave it to us to play hide-and-seek with them. It was mouserific!"

I gazed at the map with fascination. The palace had dozens of secret passages **linking** the most important rooms. That's why the key master had disappeared: he must have gone down one of the **PASSAGEWAYS** . . .

MAP OF THE SECRET PASSAGES INSIDE THE ROYAL PALACE

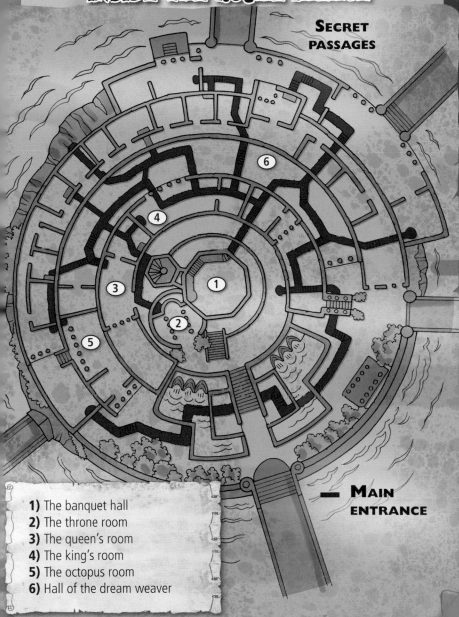

SECRET PASSAGES

1

6

4

3

2

5

— **MAIN ENTRANCE**

1) The banquet hall
2) The throne room
3) The queen's room
4) The king's room
5) The octopus room
6) Hall of the dream weaver

STOP STUFFING
YOUR SNOUT!

LOOKING carefully at the map, I noticed there was a secret passage near our rooms. An idea began to rumble around in my brain.

"What do you say we go have a look in the **key master's** room? We could find out more about him," I said.

Cheezum began to growl. **Grrr! Grufff! Grrrr!** *(I don't like that mouse!)*

"Great idea!" Thea exclaimed. "That rat seems suspicious to me, too."

Misty, who was distracted as usual, said, "There was something I wanted to tell you . . . it was very important . . . it was right on the tip of my tongue . . . but I can't remember it now."

"It'll come back to you," I replied. "For now we need to find the entrance to the **secret passage**."

"Ah, that's what I wanted to say. I figured out that the passageway is behind this octopus-shaped alcove!"

Trap, who was busy stuffing his snout with fruit, squeaked as he spat out seeds, "P-tooey

Nom, nom!

Stop stuffing your snout!

First . . . p-tooey . . . we have to find the mechanism . . . p-tooey . . . that opens it!"

Oops!

Help · · · "Stop stuffing your snout and give us a paw, why don't you?!" I squeaked. But instead he smirked and continued eating. So I went over to grab the basket of fruit, but Trap tripped me! I took a stumble and ended up banging my head against the back of the alcove. **BONK!**

Yee-ouch!

Instantly, the back of the alcove opened and I fell down . . . down . . . down . . . down . . . down . . . down . . . down . . .

down . . .

· · · uʍop

down . . .

· · · uʍop

down . . .

· · · uʍop

down . . .

Heeeeeelp!

a super-steep stairway! Crispy squid tentacles, I had found the mechanism that opened the secret passageway!

A minute or two later, my friends caught up with me, and we began to explore the **D A R K** tunnels. Until, suddenly, we heard some squeaks . . . and I recognized one of them right away. It was Aristomous, the key master!

"The QUEEN is still taking the poisoned medicine, and she is getting weaker and weaker," Aristomous was saying. "When I am king of ATLANTIS, I will make you queen! Now we need to steal the Vrill. Then tomorrow, during the ceremony of the ten kings, we will strike down the underwater pillars that hold up the palace! It must look like a terrible **TRAGEDY**."

A female squeak responded, "Yes, my lord!"

It was the maid who'd brought the queen her medicine! What was going on between her and the key master? And what in the name of string cheese was a Vrill?

But there was no time to think. We needed to

WARN the queen!

We **scurried** back down the tunnels, which were dark and scary as a cat's guts. Luckily, they were **LIT** by torches, otherwise we would have been lost forever.

We walked for a while until we finally reached the **POINT** that led to the entrance to Triton's room. We had arrived at the banquet hall.

GRRRR! RUFFFF! GRRRR!

We poked out of a secret little door hidden behind a **tapestry** and found ourselves in Triton's room. The guests were already sitting around the **banquet** table. I noticed that

Silver bowl for Cheezum

only six spots were empty: ours. Lying on the ground next to my seat, on a blue silk pillow, was a **silver bowl** for Cheezum. Flying cheese sticks, they were just waiting for us!

I **blushed** to the roots of my fur with embarrassment. We were making such a bad impression.

I crossed the room, heading straight toward the QUEEN to warn her. I bowed my snout low.

"Your Majesty, please excuse our tardiness. We received some terrible news from our island . . ."

Then I lowered my squeak so that only she could hear me. "Please, you are in **danger**! Someone is plotting against you."

The queen pretended nothing was happening, but she turned **PALE**.

She took a deep breath and said, "I present you with our guests of honor, who have arrived

What?

Your Majesty, you're in danger!

from the faraway New Mouse Citoide! **Let's celebrate!** Later in my study, we will sign an alliance treaty between our countries."

As I returned to my place, I passed the **key master**, who hissed, "I've got my eye on you, rat!"

That made Cheezum's hackles go up. **Grrrr! Rufff! Grrrrr!** (Meaning: *If you threaten my friend again, I'll bite you!*)

I managed to stop my little friend a moment

What do you want?!

Grrrr! Rufff! Grrrrr!

before he **BIT** the key master. *Calm down, little one, or we will end up in trouble!* I told him in my mind.

Except for Cheezum's outburst, the banquet continued uneventfully. The food was delicious, but I could barely eat: I was **stressed** — super stressed — in fact, the most stressed out I'd ever been!

My cousin, on the other paw, stuffed himself and burped loudly with contentment: BURP! Then he wiped his mouth on my tunic!

Come on . . .

What are you doing?

Burp!

Trap!

Finally, after what seemed like forever, the banquet was over and the queen led us to the octopus room. "Squeak to me. I'm listening! Why am I in danger?"

"The key master is plotting against you! The medicine he gave you is really **poison**," Trap cried.

"The good news is that you aren't really sick, Your Majesty," Benjamin exclaimed. "If you don't take the medicine anymore, you will get better."

The queen was upset. "The key master is betraying me? I don't believe it!"

The little prince and princess squeezed her **affectionately**. Thea took her paw to COMFORT her, and I poured her a glass of water. Misty gave her air by fanning her with a tissue.

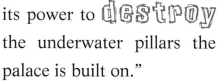

"Your Majesty, we heard him talking with your lady's maid . . . And that's not all," I continued. "The two traitors want to **destroy** the palace during the ceremony of the ten kings so that they can reign in your place!"

"And how do they plan to do it?" the QUEEN asked.

"They want to make everyone believe that it was a terrible accident. They are planning on stealing something," Misty responded **seriously**.

"They called it a Vrill," I said. "They want to use its power to **destroy** the underwater pillars the palace is built on."

We must stop them!

The queen gathered all her **STRENGTH**. She jumped to her paws and tied a crystal dagger to her waist, threw a hooded cloak over her shoulders, and cried, "For the good of the kingdom, we must stop them! I will not let **ATLANTIS** end up in the paws of such evil rodents."

She turned to us and commanded, "Follow me. I will show you our most PRECIOUS secret!"

She led us into a secret passageway that spiraled down, down, down, down, down, down, down, down, down, down until we reached a cave that held the **SECRET OF ATLANTIS** . . .

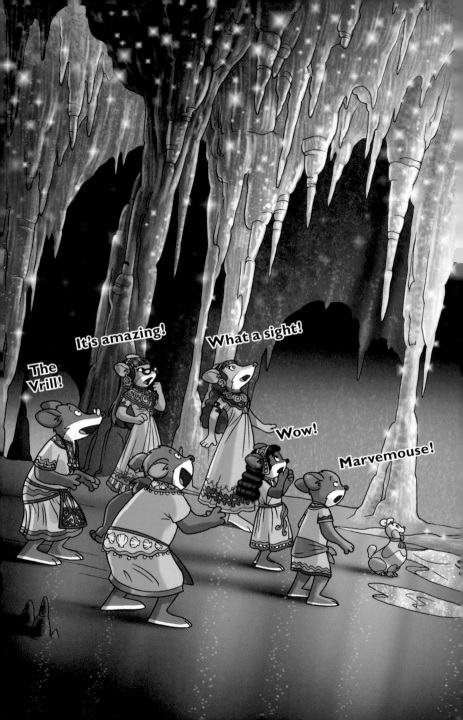

THE SECRET OF THE VRILL CRYSTAL

We found ourselves in an **enormouse** cave lit by a mysterious BLUE LIGHT. It was coming from the center of the cave, where a huge sculpture held an enormouse crystal. The queen announced, "THIS IS THE VRILL, THE HEART OF ATLANTIS!"

We all remained silent for a few moments, admiring the MYSTERIOUS crystal.

"The Vrill provides energy to the whole island. But it is very powerful," the queen continued. "If it's used for EVIL, it could not only destroy the royal palace, but also all of Atlantis!"

"We need to stop him," I exclaimed.

"We *will* stop him, Your Majesty!" cried Thea.

"You can count on us!" Misty added.

Trap did not share our attitude. He **SCURRIED** forward, trying to grab the Vrill. "I waaaant it! I just need a tiny piece! Then I can become the richest and most famous explorer of **MYSTERIES**!"

I quickly grabbed him by the tail. "Put your paws down! It's way too dangerous!" I turned to the queen. "Please forgive him, Your Majesty. He has a great **PASSION** for mysteries and, umm . . . treasures!"

Put your paws down!

But I waaaant it!

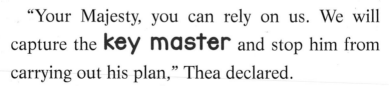

"Your Majesty, you can rely on us. We will capture the **key master** and stop him from carrying out his plan," Thea declared.

"Thank you, my **friends**!" said the queen. "But unfortunately, stopping this plan won't be enough. The spirit of peace that protects our world has been violated. If I want to protect my people, I have to put my own secret plan into action."

She pulled a precious medallion out of her tunic. It was made of the purest VRILL CRYSTAL.

She put it on the wall, which then slid open, moving along invisible tracks. On the other side there was a secret room that held a model of the city of ATLANTIS enclosed in a large crystal ball . . . that was lying on the bottom of the sea!

THE QUEEN'S MEDALLION

"I have been working on this

secret plan for a while," the queen said seriously. "**Corruption** has spread among us. I know that peace is in danger. Friends, please, defend it at all costs in your faraway land . . . Peace is the most precious resource!

"You see this model?" the queen continued. "This is what Atlantis will become. I will use the power of the VRILL to surround the city of Atlantis with a crystal ball, then I will make it . . .

SINK TO THE BOTTOM OF THE SEA!

"The rest of the world will think that a **terrible** tragedy has befallen us, but we will continue to prosper at the bottom of the **OCEAN**!"

We were struck squeakless! The queen looked us each in the eye and then asked us seriously, "Will you promise never to reveal my *secret* to anyone?"

We put our paws to our **HEARTS** and cried,

"WE PROMISE!"

Just then we heard noise coming from the VRILL cave! We were certain it was the key master.

The queen and the young prince and princess stayed hidden in the secret room. The rest of us DARTED into the cave. Thea sprang on the key master with two of her most UNBEATABLE karate moves.

Huh?

Hai-yah!

ARISTOMOUS HIT HIS SNOUT AGAINST THE WALL OF THE CAVE!

Ahhhh!

THEA DID TWO UNBEATABLE KARATE MOVES!

Aristomous wasn't expecting us or Thea's moves. He lost his **Balance** and hit his snout against the wall of the cave!

Kabang!

A huge **LUMP** began forming on the tip of his snout. While he was on the ground, the queen's guards rushed in and took him away!

"For his **BETRAYAL**, he will be sentenced

Grrr!

AN ENORMOUSE LUMP BEGAN FORMING ON HIS SNOUT.

Pbbbt!

What a bump!

THE GUARDS TIED HIM UP LIKE A HUNK OF STRING CHEESE AND TOOK HIM AWAY!

to a lifetime of exile! And my lady's maid will be banished as well," the queen said. "Now I need to put my secret plan into action before it's too late!"

"Your Majesty, unfortunately the time has come for us to say good-bye," I replied. "We must return to our distant island."

The queen **accompanied** us to the gates of Atlantis. The huge jeweled gate sparkled in the moonlight.

We said good-bye, SAD that we had to go. But the queen smiled and said, "Friends, you have the key to Atlantis! You can come and visit whenever you like. Even when the city is buried at the bottom of the **SEA**, you will still be able to enter, and we will always welcome you as friends!"

The queen gave us each a hug, and then she **returned** to the royal palace to carry out her secret plan and save her people.

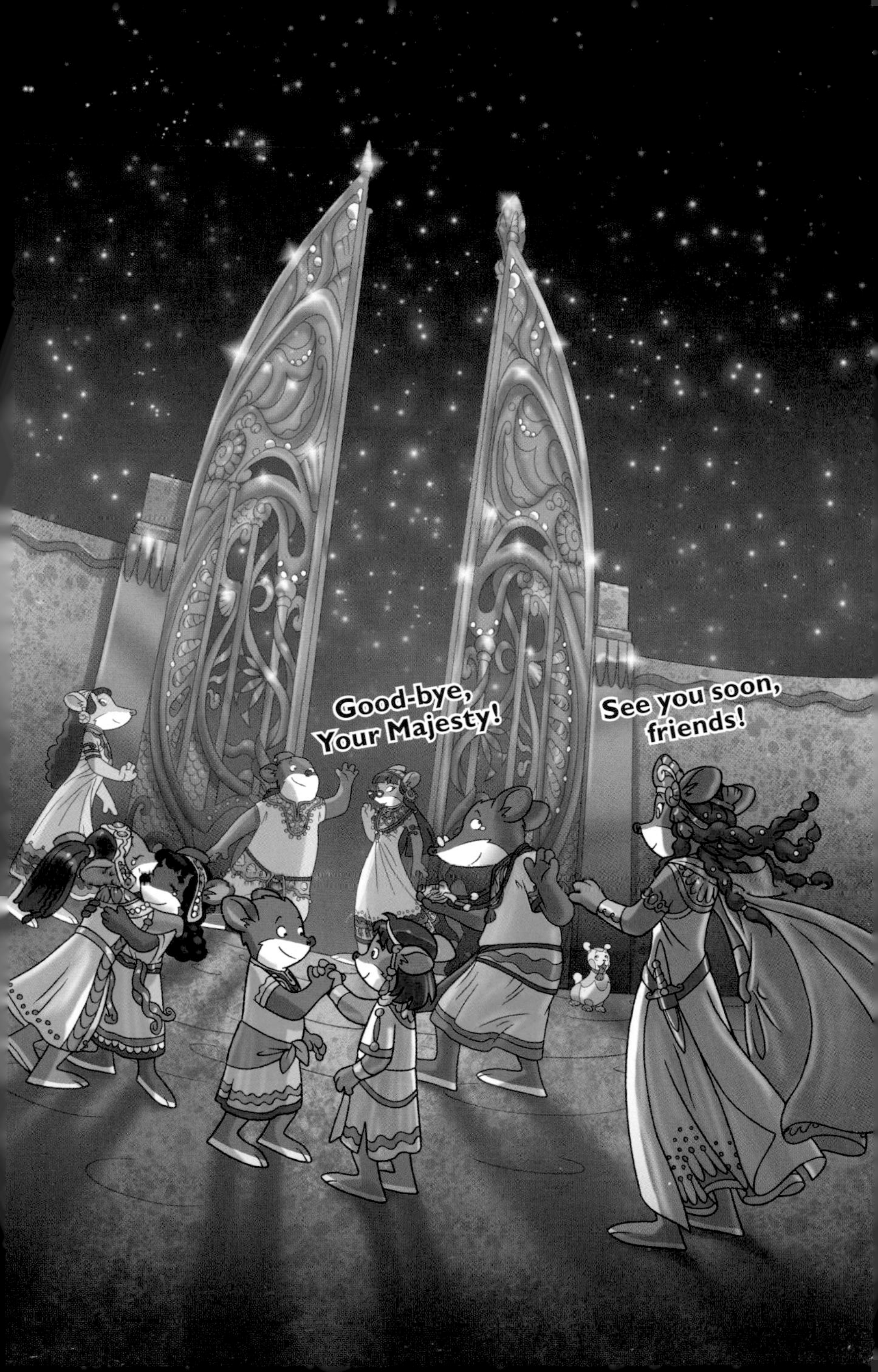
Good-bye, Your Majesty!
See you soon, friends!

As soon as I was sure we were alone, I pressed the small button on my octopus-shaped ring, and the Time Tentacle 2000 returned to its normal size.

My heart was full of sadness, but I was also happy that we had helped the queen of Atlantis keep the peace in her kingdom. And so we climbed aboard, ready to reach our next destination: **STONEHENGE AT THE TIME OF THE DRUIDS!**

The journey to
STONEHENGE

STONEHENGE, HERE WE COOOOOME!

As we climbed on board, I turned around one last time. Soon there would be no trace of the amazing city of **ATLANTIS**. To you the truth, I was about to shed a tear. You see, I can be a little cheesy sometimes!

Misty was getting a little sentimental, too. Wavering whiskers, we were a lot alike! She pawed me a tissue, sobbing, "Let's stay **strong**, Stilton, my dear mouse! It's okay. Atlantis will continue in peace at the bottom of the sea."

Waaaaaah!

I dried my eyes and **sighed**. "You're right, Misty. I'll miss

Atlantis, but the important thing is that it will carry on in peace forever!"

"And it's thanks in part to us that **ATLANTIS** will live on, right, Uncle G?" Benjamin added.

I stroked his ears affectionately. "Of course, Benjamin! It's mostly thanks to you and Bugsy. Because of you, we had the map of the **SECRET PASSAGES**."

"We got this, Benjamin! We are the best!" Bugsy yelped enthusiastically.

"That's enough of all this sweetness and sobbing," Trap interrupted. "We need to make like a cheese wheel and roll! There are mysteries waiting for us in the **land of Druids**." He began scurrying to the command center, crying, **"STONEHENGE, HERE WE COOOOOME!"**

The Time Tentacle 2000 sped forward, and we were off! Soon it began to bounce **UP** and **DOWN** ...

Squeak, what a shake-up!

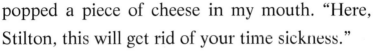

Here!

Almost at once, I began to feel 𝕥𝕚𝕞𝕖 𝕤𝕚𝕔𝕜. I was terribly queasy, but Misty quickly popped a piece of cheese in my mouth. "Here, Stilton, this will get rid of your time sickness."

Then she put on her **TIME GLASSES**. "Come on, Stilton, my dear mouse, open your eyes and get to work! You need to make an effort if you want to stay alive. The time of the druids was very dangerous, you know."

Just like the last two times, Misty pressed a button, and a panel slid down from the walls of the Time Tentacle 2000's command center.

I care deeply about my **fur**, so I looked at the panel very carefully. There was a circle of rocks in the distance, and some Druids were meeting in a thick forest during a full **moon**. They were cutting mistletoe from some bushes.

Rotten rats' teeth, what a peculiar time we were heading to! Squeeeak, I feared it would too **EERIE** for a 'fraidy mouse like me!

My whiskers began to quiver with fright. Trap, on the other paw, was **REJOICING**. "What a mysterious place: Stonehenge . . . the Druids . . . We are sure to discover great material for the show! Get ready, Cuz. We are once more in search of **MYSTERIES**!"

"Trap, remember that we are on a *peace* mission. We aren't here for your show!" I protested.

Trap **WAVED** my contract under my snout.

What a mysterious place!

Brrrrrr . . .

"Geronimo, remember that you signed this! And that you're my victim . . . I mean, assistant! In case you don't remember . . ."

I rolled my eyes. "I know, I know. I will have to **wash** your socks for the rest of my life. You don't have to keep reminding me!"

Thea broke up our ratfight. "That's enough, you two. Cut it out! It's time for Misty to **tell** us about life during the Druids' time. We need to prepare if we want our mission to succeed. After all, we are here to learn how to keep the peace from the peoples of the past."

My sister turned to Misty with an encouraging **smile**. "Go on, my dear. It's your turn!"

Misty began to rummage in her bag, muttering, "I had prepared some **notes**, but . . . where did I put them?"

Where did I put them?

When she finally found them, she began explaining everything about the **Druids.**

215

Misty's Notes on the Druids

THE DRUIDS

The Druids were powerful Celtic religious figures, a class of wise men who were the keepers of knowledge and tradition that were passed down orally. They were prophets, healers, and advisors, and they held authority in war and peace. They also acted as judges and would rule on disputes between people.

DRUID MEANS . . .

The word druid is linked to the Latin word druides; some scholars believe it comes from the Old Irish word druí and possibly to the Old English word trēow, meaning "tree."

OTHER WISE MEN

Among the Druids there were also bards (bardoi), who were singers and storytellers, and the Vates (ouateis), who were seers.

CELTIC SOCIETY

Celtic society had a pyramid structure. At the top were the tribe leaders and the Druids, who had all the power. In the center were the free and semi-free peasants, and at the bottom were the slaves.

• Remember to tell Uncle Paws to remind me to . . . what? Oh no, I can't remember!

The CELTIC RELIGION was based on concepts like the immortality of the soul and love for nature, in particular for some plants like the oak, which was considered sacred.

CELTIC GODS

The Druids passed down Celtic mythology through oral tradition. Among the major gods we can recall Lugh, a god who knew how to play the harp and write poetry, make houses, forge iron, and win in combat. There's also Odin (also known as Wotan), who was considered a war god and a protector of heroes.

THE CELTS AND COURAGE

According to the Romans, the Celts weren't afraid of anything because they believed in the immortality of the soul. They believed that after death, a man's soul passed to another body. This made the Celts more courageous, especially in battle!

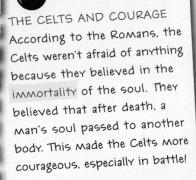

Remember to tell Geronimo he has nice whiskers!

Boing! Boing! Boing! Bada-Boing!

I was still listening to Misty when the Time Tentacle 2000 made three jumps, then one last huge jump, and we landed with a bang.

BOING! BOING! BOING!

Greasy cat guts, what an **awful** landing!

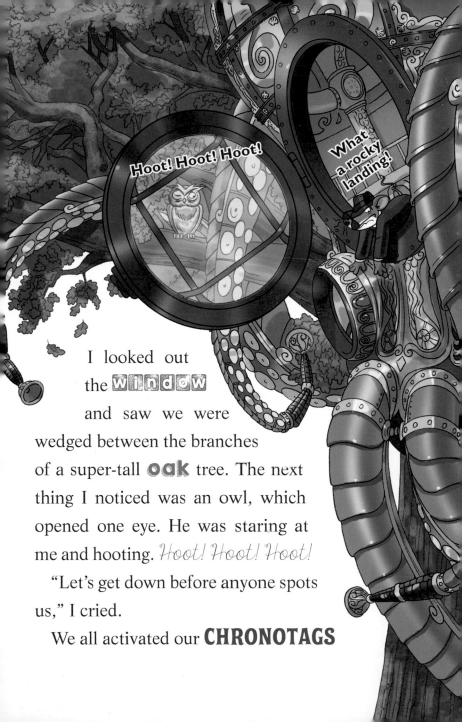

I looked out the **window** and saw we were wedged between the branches of a super-tall **oak** tree. The next thing I noticed was an owl, which opened one eye. He was staring at me and hooting. *Hoot! Hoot! Hoot!*

"Let's get down before anyone spots us," I cried.

We all activated our **CHRONOTAGS**

Misty's Notes about Celtic Fashion

MEN'S FASHION

The Celts wore multicolored clothing, mostly tunics that were embroidered with various colors and pants called braccae. They also wore cloaks that were striped or plaid and tied together by a clasp at the shoulders. On their feet they wore soft leather boots.

What did they look like? The Celts were tall. They had fair skin, and they would lighten their hair color by washing it with lime juice. Then they would comb it back from their foreheads and pull it up.

TORC
The Celts wore torcs around their necks. A torc would wrap around the neck and open in the front. It was often made with gold and silver to balance the power of the metals.

WOMEN'S FASHION

Women generally wore big dresses taken in at the waist by belts with fabric or with leather clasps. In the winter, they covered themselves with shawls or long cloaks. They particularly loved jewelry, like bracelets, which they wore around their wrists and ankles, and pins, which were used to hold together clothes and cloaks.

and pressed the button for **STONEHENGE MODE**. A moment later, we were dressed in Celtic fashion! I pressed the **SHRINK** button, and the Time Tentacle 2000 turned into a ring. I slipped it onto my finger and we hurried outside. Phewwww, we barely avoided getting shrunk!

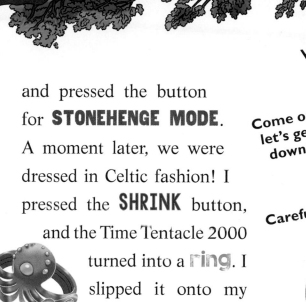

We carefully climbed down the oak on a vine. Squeeeak, I felt so dizzy! My paws were slick with sweat. Which is how the ring *slipped* off my paw and fell to the ground. **Plink!**

As soon as I touched

Wow!

Come on, let's get down!

Careful . . .

We're almost there . . .

Come on, Cuz!

Aaack! The riiiing . . .

THE TIME TENTACLE 2000

down, I kneeled and kissed the ground, **sobbing** with relief. "I'm aliiiiive! I'm still aliiiiiive!"

Then Thea **knocked** on my forehead. "Gerry Berry, calm down, okay? We have to look for the **ring** or we'll never be able to get home."

Crusty cheddar chunks, Thea was right! We all began to look for the ring, but it was pretty **dark** under the trees, and the forest floor was thick with ferns and

Look carefully!

It's not over here!

fallen leaves. I began fretting about whether we'd ever find it.

Then I got an idea. *You're an electronic brain made of quantico-cheese molecules! Tell me, where did the Time Tentacle 2000 fall?* I asked Cheezum telepathically.

In response, he licked my snout. **Slurp! Lick! Gruff! Slurp . . .** *(It's obvious, mouse! Considering the mass of the ring, the gravitational pull, the wind, and friction, the ring fell here, right under your paw!)*

Umm . . .

Where did it go?

I lifted my paw, but . . . there was no sign of the ring! Anxiously, I began to rummage around . . .

. . . and that's when I bumped into a rodent who was as tall and thick as a cheese churn. He had two thick, cheese-colored whiskers and a stern expression on his snout.

"Lose something, rat?" the rodent thundered.

"Well . . . actually . . . I—I—I did lose a little something . . . a little ring . . . and I really like it . . .

Did you lose something, rat?

BANG!

224

you didn't see it around here? It's shaped like an octopus . . ." I **Stammered**.

"Me? I didn't find **anything**," he replied.

At that moment, I looked down and noticed he had the Time Tentacle 2000 around his finger! I tried to ask him about it tactfully. "Well, my ring looks **JUST** like yours. I mean, it **really, really, really** looks like yours. In fact, it is **practically** identical to yours . . ."

"Are you suggesting I took your ring, rat?" he thundered.

SQUEEEAK, I WAS TERRIFIED!

THIS IS FEAR!
TRUE FEAR!

The rodent loomed as large as a **cheetah**, and as menacing as a mongoose. He could make me into mousemeat in the blink of a cat's eye! I turned as pale as rotten mozzarella. Squeeeak! My WHISKERS began to shake like mad, and my **tongue** stuck to the roof of my mouth. "H-h-help! Don't m-m-make me into m-m-mousemeat!" I stammered.

He looked at me. "Why are your whiskers shaking? Why are you as pale as the moon? Are you sick?"

Why are your whiskers shaking?

H-h-help!

"Oh, that's not sickness, it's **FEAR**." Trap snickered. "True fear!"

The rodent opened his eyes wide. "**FEAR?** What is this 'fear'? I've never heard that word."

"**FEAR** means . . . being terribly afraid. And now put down my brother, you furface!" Thea said.

Cheezum growled, Grrrr! Grrrrr! Grrrrruffff! (*Leave that mouse be, you ugly swamp-rat snout!*)

"Leave him be, lard ball!" Bugsy and Benjamin yelled.

"Umm . . . the *rest* of you aren't afraid, I see," the rodent said. "*He* is, though! So he's going to come meet **AIDAN**, our leader and my dad!"

Then he tossed me over his shoulders like a sack of potatoes and stomped off to his village.

My friends and Cheezum followed us, crying,

"PUT HIM DOWN NOW!" RUFF! GRRRRRUFFF! *(Mouse, I'll save you!)* But the rodent, Maddix, wouldn't let me go.

We reached the destination at **sunrise**. Though I was still hanging upside down over Maddix's back, I noticed that the **village** was waking up. Female rodents were feeding the hens, who were scratching about in the grass or lighting **FIRES** to prepare the first meal of the day.

The artisans' shops were showing their wares: splendid metal and **jewels**, shields, decorated helmets, dishware, and multicolored fabrics.

The hunters were getting ready to leave the village, and the warriors were **PAINTING** their faces a strange blue color. Squeeeak, they were really **scary**!

Finally, we reached a hut that was bigger than the others. Maddix released me, and I fell flat on my snout.

THE CELTIC VILLAGE

The Celts were first and foremost
BREEDERS of pigs, cows, and
oxen, and they produced
meat and milk. Among their
domesticated animals were
sheep, which were precious for
their wool, and goats and horses. The fur of these animals
was used to make objects and clothing.

AGRICULTURE also made up an important part of
the daily life of the Celts. Barley was one of the most
important plants they cultivated.

 The Celts' CRAFTSMANSHIP was
very developed. The blacksmiths and
goldsmiths were very skilled artisans:
they decorated
weapons, jewelry, and utensils.

The Celts were also
AGGRESSIVE WARRIORS. They
fought tirelessly and considered
honor to be the most precious
treasure.

KABONK!

Dad, come look!

Ouch, my snout!

Then he called, "Dad! I finally found a rat who knows what FEAR is! He's an expert — all his friends say so!"

A mouse emerged out of the hut. He had the same blond whiskers and the huge, hulking body as Maddix.

He looked me up and down. "You know something about fear, rat?"

Trap snickered. "Of course. My cousin is the world **champion** of fear!"

"Then join us in battle! And since you know so much about it, you can make our **opponents** feel fear!"

"But I . . . actually . . . er . . . I'm an expert in being afraid, not in making mice afraid," I tried to explain.

Then everything turned black, and I **fainted**!

I'm good at being afraid . . .

Huh?

What is he doing? Fainting?

PAWS OFF THE GOLD SICKLE!

I woke up a little while later to find Misty holding a piece of **super-stinky** Celtic cheese under my nose. Moldy Brie on a baguette, it stank like a dirty sock that'd been left to rot in a barrel of rotten fish.

Yuck! What an appalling stench!

I was about to faint again when Thea gave me a smack on either side of my snout. "Now's not the time to faint, Gerry Berry! We need to get to the Time Tentacle 2000, or we will be PRISONERS of the past forever!"

Only then did I fully wake up and look around. We were in a strange hut. Bunches of scented **herbs** hung from the ceiling, and above the door there was a fern branch. Leaning on a ledge

was a magnificent **GOLDEN SICKLE**.

As I **GAZED** curiously at the sickle, Trap grabbed it, crying, "I'm going to **snatch** this thing here! It's an authentic Druid sickle! This is going to be a great reveal for my show!"

I was about to **PROTEST** when I felt a whack on the side of my snout. Yeee-ouch!!! Then a squeak behind us barked, "PAWS OFF THE GOLD SICKLE!"

Rubbing my aching snout, I turned around slowly and saw a tall, skinny rodent. "I'm **Druidix**, the Great Druid, and that is my golden sickle! How dare you?!" he snapped.

With my whiskers **trembling** in fear, I apologized. "Excuse us, Great Druid. I didn't mean to **snatch** the sickle."

He stared at me. "Ah, I know who you are. You're the expert in **FEAR**!"

I burst into tears. "Great Druidix, there's been a terrible mistake! I don't know how to **scare**

Yes, I'm scared, I'm afraid, I'm terrified!

Umm . . .

mice! I only know how to be scared! Oh, great Druidix, can you help me? Otherwise I'll be mousemeat . . ."

My outburst seemed to catch Druidix by surprise. "Umm . . . let's see . . . I must think for a moment . . ." Then he turned and scurried away.

"Cuz, I think you're mousemeat," Trap said. "So tell me, have you written your **will**? Have you

thought about who you're going to leave your cheese rind collection to? And *The Rodent's Gazette*? Let me give you some good advice: Just leave it all to meeee!"

Now I'd really had it up to my whiskers. "Stop it, everyone! I have no intention of becoming **mousemeat**!"

"Okay, then, brother," Thea said, "you have no choice: You must learn how to . . .

MAKE MICE AFRAID!"

A SCARY SNOUT!

"Come on, Geronimo, I'll help you train," my sister went on encouragingly. "Try to make a **SCARY SNOUT**!"

I tried my best, I swear I did, but Thea just burst out laughing.

"I said **SCAAARRRY**! You need to try harder! Come on, make a *scarier* snout!" she urged me.

I tried again . . . and again . . . and again . . . and **AGAIN**! But nothing worked. I'd contort my whiskers into some horrible expression, and my sister would burst out laughing. Each time, her laugh got louder and louder until she began to **roll** on the ground, roaring with hilarity!

Finally, with tears in her eyes from laughing so hard, she said, "Geronimo, you really are a hopeless case! You just aren't capable of making

 Heh, heh, heh!

 Hee, hee, hee!

Ha, ha, ha!

Arrgh! Booooo! Umm . . .

Harrrr!

ATTEMPT 1

ATTEMPT 2

ATTEMPT 3

ATTEMPT 4

Argh . . .

Aaah!

Blaggghh!

Psssst!

ATTEMPT 5

ATTEMPT 6

ATTEMPT 7

ATTEMPT 8

Hoo, hoo, hoo!
Ha, ha, ha!
Ho, ho, ho!
Heh, heh,
heh!

Uggghhh!

Grrrr!

Geronimo, you
really make
me laugh!

ATTEMPT 9

ATTEMPT 10

anymouse afraid! But you've given me an **idea** . . ."

Thea leaned in and whispered, "When you're

Pssst . . . psssssst . . . out on the battlefield, you

must . . . psst . . . pssst . . .

psssssst . . . understand?"

"Huh? Do you really think that will work?" I asked skeptically.

"I'm not sure. But I am very, very sure that we have

no other choice," my sister replied.

"L-l-let's hope it w-w-works . . ."

I stammered. My teeth were chattering with terror!

Just then Maddix entered the hut, lifted me on his shoulders like a sack of **potatoes**, and carried me away.

A few minutes later, he DUMPED me right in the middle of two armies lined up for

battle. "COME ON, MAKE OUR ENEMIES AFRAID, OR I'LL TURN YOU INTO MOUSEMEAT!"

"Come on, Gerry Berry, show them what you've got!" Thea hollered.

So I started doing what she'd told me to do earlier. I tried my best, making all the MOST TERRIFYING snouts I could. I even tried to make scary sounds.

"Grrrrrr! Grrrrrr! Ooooooo! Booooooo!"

HO, HO, HO!

HA, HA, HA!

HEH, HEH, HEH!

HEE, HEE, HEE!

HA, HA, HA!

HO, HO, HO

For a moment every single mouse fell silent. They all looked at one another and then . . . everyone — and I do mean *everyone* — burst out **laughing**. They were laughing so hard, they laid their weapons on the ground and began to **roll** around. Thea's plan had worked . . . *maybe*!

HA HA HA!
THE MAGICAL POWER OF LAUGHTER

The two opposing armies continued to laugh hysterically for quite a while. Every so often, one of the warriors would come up for air and say, "That mouse is **hilarious**!"

"I've never seen such a **ridicumouse** rodent!"

"I can't take it anymore, he's too **funny**!"

HA! HA, HA, HA! HEH, HEH, HEH! HO! HO, HO! HU, HU, HU! HI, HI, HI! HU, HI!

Then Aidan and the leader of the **enemies** approached. *Moldy mozzarella, now they'll slice me like Swiss cheese!* I thought. I closed my **EYES**, ready to become mousemeat . . .

Am I mousemeat
or am I not mousemeat?
Squeeak!
What a cat-astophe!
Help . . .
Holey cheese, this
won't end well!

But instead . . .

Instead, the two leaders patted each other on the tail, saying, "I don't feel like fighting, do you?"

"Me neither!"

"What do you say we have a **feast**?"

"Great idea!"

"Dear ex-enemy, what are we going to do with this mouse?" **AIDAN** said. "Should we turn him to mousemeat or what?"

The Great Druid intervened. "Everyone, stop! This mouse is not to be touched! Today he stopped a battle, and so he will stay alive. In fact, he deserves a **PRize**."

"And so it shall be," Aidan agreed. "Today is your **lucky** day, rat! What do you want as a prize? Squeak!"

"Uncle G, the **riiiiing**," Benjamin whispered.

He was right. This was our chance to get the Time Tentacle 2000 back!

"As my prize I would like . . . that OCTOPUS-shaped ring that Maddix has on his finger!" I declared.

Maddix took the ring off his finger and grudgingly pawed it to me.

"This doesn't end here, **RAT**! Sooner or later I'll get my paws on you and turn you into mousemeat . . ." he muttered.

But Aidan was satisfied. "GOOD! Now let's think about the FEAST . . ."

He put his paw around his former ENEMY, and the two leaders went off paw in paw, having a friendly conversation about the menu for the feast.

"I will bring TWELVE wild boars!"

"And I will bring FIFTY bear legs ready to roast!"

"Hooray, now we eat!" Trap rejoiced.

"Did you hear that? We're not fighting anymore! Now we're feasting!!!" a soldier from one army said to a soldier from the other.

HOORAY FOR FEASTS! HOORAY!
HOORAY FOR BEAR LEGS! HOORAY!

As I put the ring on my finger, my friends ran to **hug** me. We were saved! We could go home!

"Congratulations, mouse, you have just been nominated Druid apprentice!" Aidan told me.

"Huh? Wh-what? How? When? And most important . . . why?" I stammered.

"Because you knew how to make peace between two armies like a real Druid, but mostly because you have the power of LaUGHteR! That will be very useful to you," Druidix responded. "But you must try your hardest and study for at least twenty years."

I imagined what my life as a Druid would be like. "Oh, Great Druid, I am **honored** by your proposal, but . . . umm . . . I don't have twenty years to spare. I must return to my island to keep the peace among mice."

"If it is to bring peace, then go ahead," he said solemnly.

"There is nothing more important than peace: You must keep it and defend it at any price."

Trap PINCHED my snout and whispered in my ear, "Cuz — I mean, assistant — we can't leave yet! First we need to uncover the MYSTERIES of Stonehenge! Come on, ask him about Stonehenge, or you will have to wash my socks for the rest of your life . . . remember, you signed a contract!"

THE POWER OF LAUGHTER
Those who are able to laugh and make others laugh have great power, because laughing isn't just good for your soul, it's also good for your health. Laughter can warm the coldest hearts, it can smooth over arguments, and calm souls. Learn to laugh and you'll live better!

PEACE

Many people live in the world, each one different from the next.

Even our **natural environments** are very different: some people live in hot weather, others live in the cold, some live in the country and others in the city, some live in huts and others live in skyscrapers.

Each population has its own **customs** and **habits**, its own history, and traditions, and religion. These differences have often led to conflict over the centuries.

No one civilization is superior or inferior to another: We are all just **different**. This diversity allows us to exchange and share: it makes us curious, it stimulates us, it lets us discover new things, and it makes us richer.

If people have different **ideas**, they should talk to one another and respect those ideas. If they do that, they can find a way to get along. **Nothing is more important than peace!**

THE MYSTERYYYY
OF . . . STONEHENGE!

I didn't dare ask the Great Druid to tell me his secrets. I would rather have washed Trap's socks (even if they are **super stinky**!). But luckily, Benjamin was far more brave than me. He stepped forward, cleared his throat, and asked, "Druidix, can you please tell us the secrets of Stonehenge? We have come from very far away to discover them."

Druidix smiled. "Being **CURIOUS** is a good thing for little mice like you! All right, since you — and not that rude rat who wanted to paw at my gold sickle — asked, I will tell you the **MYSTERIES** of Stonehenge. Follow me!"

He led us through the forest, explaining the mystery of Stonehenge as we scurried along . . .

THE MYSTERY OF STONEHENGE

Some believe that we Druids built Stonehenge using magic. We let them believe this so they fear us more. But the truth is that this ring of stones was built between 3100 and 1600 BC and already existed when we arrived in these parts. We carry out our sacred ceremonies inside the forest, in clearings between oak trees.

Stonehenge is not our temple, although we do use it to gaze at the stars! It is much more than that. It is a mystery because no one knows how it was made or by whom.

We scurried along for hours until at last we stood in front of that mysterious **ring of stones.**

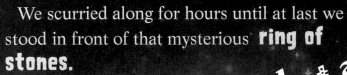

Good Gouda, what a marvemouse sight!

"But if you Druids didn't build Stonehenge, who did?" Benjamin asked.

"It is a mystery that not even I know the answer to," Druidix responded seriously.

We stayed there for a long while in silence, looking at those **Great** carved **STONES**.

Then, when Night began to fall, Druidix said good-bye. "Now I will leave you, but you should stay here tonight. Perhaps in a dream these stones will tell you their most *mysterious* secrets . . ."

We lay down under the starry sky and **fell asleep** . . .

I dreamed that a voice was calling me. **"GERONIMOOOO! WAKE UUPPP!"**

"Who's there? Who is it?" I asked.

"It's us, the stones! We are alive and we remember everything . . ."

"What do you remember?" I asked eagerly.

"We were **BUILT** by an ancient people called . . ."

Suddenly, someone **PULLED** my whisker, and I twitched.

A moment later, someone **PULLED** another whisker . . . and I twitched again.

Finally, I opened my **EYES** and saw that it was

my cousin Trap. "Huh? What? The stones . . . I was just about to find out . . ." I said.

But Trap PULLED my whiskers again. "Wake up, Cousinkins, we have guests!"

I hid behind one of the stones and peered into the forest. Maddix was STORMING toward us. "You thieving mouse, where are you? If I find you, I'll turn you into mousemeat, and then I'll get my ring back! I liked that ring, you know!"

As Trap woke the others, I pressed the small button that would make the Time Tentacle 2000 return to normal size. We jumped on board, and I immediately pressed the button for our next destination . . .

NEW MOUSE CITY IN THE FUTURE!

The journey to
THE FUTURE!

WELCOME TO NEW MOUSE CITY!

As the Time Tentacle 2000 **BOUNCED** us all around as usual, a thousand questions rattled through my brain:

WHAT WILL NEW MOUSE CITY BE LIKE IN THE FUTURE?

WILL MY HOUSE STILL BE THERE?

WILL THE RODENT'S GAZETTE STILL BE AROUND?

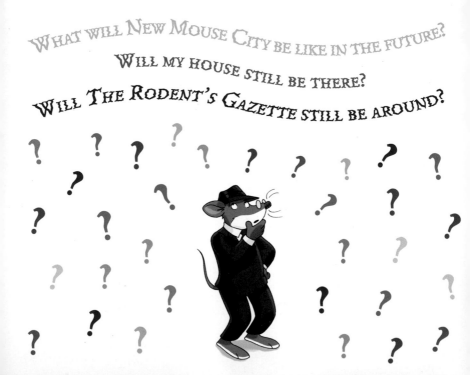

Who knows? Who knows? Who knows?

Then Misty pinched my tail. "Wake up, Geronimo, my dear! We need to change our clothes."

"I can't wait to find out how they dress in the future," Bugsy exclaimed.

"We'll find out soon enough. We just need to press the **CHRONOTAG** and set it to future mode," Thea replied.

A moment later, we were dressed in super-technological suits. I wondered whether rodents would really dress like this in the future. We would find out as soon as we reached our destination!

After the usual little jumps and big jumps that produced the usual feeling that I was about to lose my cheese, the Time Tentacle 2000 stopped. I pressed the usual button, and we scurried out before we could be shrunk along with the Time Tentacle 2000. Only then did I look around.

We were in the middle of New Mouse City in the future!

We hid behind a bush to finish fixing our **outfits**, which turned out to be very well equipped. Rancid rat hairs, Professor von Volt was really a super **SCIENTIST**!

When we were ready, Bugsy exclaimed, **"Check us out. We look good!"**

We're in the future!

"These are the rat's pajamas!" Benjamin squeaked enthusiastically.

My heart was pounding with excitement as we scampered through the streets of the city.

New Mouse City looked really rattastic! The air was clean, and the sky was clear and blue. The cars flew silently and speedily, and the streets were lush green fields! Along the streets

Good morning!

Hello!

What a beautiful day!

the early risers were exercising, **running**, and enjoying power scampers.

"Okay, so when do we eat? I'm starved!" Trap grumbled, rubbing his belly.

I was **HUNGRY**, too. "Are you in the mood for a seven-cheese pizza? Topped with a nice cream-cheese-and-mozzarella smoothie?"

"Yes! Bring on all seven cheeses!" Bugsy and Benjamin said eagerly.

We headed to the street to the spot where, in the present, the best restaurant in the city is located — the Golden Cheese. 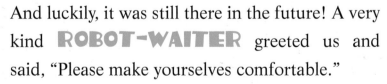 And luckily, it was still there in the future! A very kind **ROBOT-WAITER** greeted us and said, "Please make yourselves comfortable."

But That's Stilton, Geronimo Stilton!

The thoughtful waiter led us to our table. But before he did, he pulled our WHISKERS and passed them through a SCANNER. Then, instead of showing us a menu, he projected holograms of the daily specials.

Mmm, yummy!

Everything looked so delicious!

We began by ordering a delicious appetizer of aged cheese tarts. We also asked for SKEWERS with grilled Gouda and melted cheddar, a cheese **pie** with Gorgonzola and fresh mozzarella, a soup made of Swiss, and for dessert, little cookies made from sweet cream cheese and chocolate!

But when we were finished ordering, the waiter shook his snout. "I'm sorry, sir, you mice can't order this food. You see, this much food exceeds the caloric quantity you're permitted each day. It would be really unhealthy!"

Cheezum licked my snout. Slurp! Ruff! Slurp!

"But we're hungry!" I protested.

The waiter was unwavering. "Then you must do some healthy exercises first! Follow me, please!"

He led us to a corner of the restaurant, where a row of rodents was pedaling on bicycles.

"Make yourself comfortable! The energy produced by your pedaling will be used to power New Mouse City's **ENERGY-SAVING** program."

I shrugged my shoulders in despair. I had no choice. I began to pedal as Trap kept time for me.

I *PEDALED . . . AND PEDALED . . . AND PEDALED*. Meanwhile, I brooded over the fact that New Mouse City in the future was really serious about protecting the health of its **CITIZENS** . . .

All of a sudden, a little mouse pointed at me and cried, "Look, that's Stilton, Geronimo Stilton!"

The ratlet's mother smiled. "Impossible, my little cheese nip! You have too much imagination! How could that be Geronimo Stilton, the famouse hero who brought PEACE to Mouse Island? He and his friends lived many, many, many years ago!"

"But it's him, it's really him! He looks just like

the rat in the statue in front of *The Rodent's Gazette* . . . I'm sure of it, Mom!" the little mouse insisted.

My fur flushed **red** with embarrassment. "Umm, in fact, I do look a lot like that ancient rodent . . ."

Then I covered my snout with my hood and scurried over to my friends at the table. "We need to go! I've been recognized," I panted.

We quickly **LEFT** the restaurant, yelling to the waiter, "We're not hungry after all! Thanks anyway!"

We scampered over to number 17. Holey cheese, *The Rodent's Gazette* was still there! And right in front there was a large **statue**. We tried to blend into the crowd of rodents and listen to what the **tour guide** was saying.

"This is the old headquarters of *The Rodent's Gazette*, which has been turned into a **museum**

of peace. Next door is the newspaper's new headquarters, **designed** by the famouse architect Mousiford Tracer," the tour guide was saying.

"In front of the museum is this statue dedicated to the

peacekeepers: Geronimo Stilton; his sister, Thea; his cousin Trap; his nephew Benjamin, and their friends Bugsy Wugsy and Misty and Paws von Volt. Back in ancient times, they worked together to stop a **GREAT WAR** between cats and rats from breaking out . . ."

Jumping gerbil babies! In that moment, everything became clear as cheese broth. Our future depends on the choices that we make day by day in the present!

I whispered to my friends, "Let's go home! Now that we've seen what New Mouse City is like in the FUTURE, we have an important mission to carry out."

We ran to the New Mouse City HARBOR, and while no one was looking, I pressed the tiny button on my ring.

The Time Tentacle 2000 returned to its normal size, and we jumped in and pressed the button that would take us to our final destination: New Mouse City in the present!

HOME AT LAST!

The journey to
NEW MOUSE CITY!

BACK HOME IN NEW MOUSE CITY

As always, the Time Tentacle 2000 began to hop **UP** and **DOWN** and **UP** and **DOWN** and **UP** and **DOWN** ... **UP** and **DOWN** and **UP** and **DOWN** and **UP** and **DOWN** ... Oh, my poor stomach!

My fur turned greener than a lizard in spring. I was sure I was about to get another glimpse of the Christmas dinner I had eaten three years ago!

I consoled myself by reflecting that that was the last time I would suffer from **time sickness**. Soon we would be in New Mouse City in the present!

Luckily, this time the trip was a lot shorter than usual. After just a few minutes of bouncing (*and*

I mean **serious bouncinG**! *It was awful, let me tell you!*) the Time Tentacle 2000 stopped.

I **stumbled** out and found myself in Professor von Volt's laboratory. The **Mega Octo-Portal** had moved from Bimini to the coast of New Mouse City!

The professor greeted us with a smile. "Welcome home, friends! Come, I've made a **cheese** lunch for you. You must be tired. Traveling through time is exhausting . . ."

"Finally, we can eeeeaaaat!" Trap shouted.

"It feels like I haven't eaten in centuries! No, MILLENNIA!"

While we all stuffed their snouts, I told Professor von Volt everything that happened on our incredible *journey through time*.

When I was done telling of our adventures to Atlantis, Stonehenge, and the future, the professor asked, "So, Geronimo, what have you learned from the peoples of the past about peace?"

"We've learned that peace is the most precious resource and we need to be ready to face down any threat in order to defend it," I replied.

"Then, Geronimo, you must scurry over to city hall at once," the professor said in his most serious squeak. "The mayor is meeting with representatives from Cat Island. They want to declare war on us mice!"

"It's an emergency, friends! We must stop them," I hollered. "Thea, Bugsy, Benjamin, run to *The Rodent's Gazette* and prepare a special edition about the importance of peace. I will go to city hall to try and keep the peace . . ."

"Stilton, I'm coming with you, don't worry!" declared Misty.

Trap pinched my ear. "I'm coming with you, too, Cuz. I need you alive for our show tonight! Are you reeeaaady?"

Cheezum licked my snout. Slurp! Lick! (*I'm coming with you, too!*)

Thanks, friends.

Slurp!

And so we said good-bye to our friends, and left the secret laboratory, and . . . **plunk!** . . . found ourselves in the waters of the New Mouse City harbor!

Brrr! It was freezing!

We swam to shore and raced toward city hall, soaking wet and covered in algae. We looked just like **swamp monsters**! I began to sneeze nonstop: "Achoo! Achoo! Achoo!"

Misty passed me her pawkerchief (*which was soaking wet!*) so I could blow my nose. "Poor Stilton! You really are a **cheese puff** . . ."

When we reached city hall, I was covered like a swamp monster, I stank like rotting fish, and my nose was as red as a lobster!

Squeak!

Answer on page 308.

STBOP, EBERYONE, LBET'S MBAKE PBEACE!

I burst into the assembly hall, **shouting**: "Stbop . . . eberyone, lbet's mbake . . . *achoo!* . . . pbeace!" (I meant to say, "Stop, everyone, let's make peace!" but I was terribly cold and could barely squeak!)

Everyone stopped **YELLING** for a moment and turned toward me. They just stared . . . and stared . . . and stared . . . and then they all burst out laughing!

"**HA, HA, HA! HEH, HEH, HEH! HO, HO, HO!**"

"What a ridicumouse rodent! This is too funny!"

"Well done, Stilton, my dear. You used the **power of laughter** again," Misty said admiringly.

I decided to take advantage of the fact that

everyone had stopped yelling for a moment. I jumped on a chair and began to squeak in defense of **PEACE**.

"Dear rodent frienbds and dear . . . umm . . . feline frienbds, I know there is a good reason for the **conflict** between us, but let's try to find a solution together!"

I turned to **Bengal Longhair**, the king of the pirate cats. My tail was trembling with fear, but I held firm. "Umm, Your Hbighness, wbhy do you want to declare war against Mouse Island?"

Bengal Longhair snickered and licked his whiskers. "To eat you all, ratface! Unfortunately,

BENGAL LONGHAIR

III of Catatonia is the third king of the Catatonian dynasty. He rules Cat Island. He is a clever, aggressive, unprincipled cat — plus he is lazy and very, very greedy!

the **fish** around our ocean are going extinct, so we intend to gobble up all the mice on the island.

"Why, I could start with you and **eat** you as an appetizer! You're a mouse . . . but you stink like a rotten fish. Yum . . . you look quite tasty!"

Squeak, how terrifying! That nasty cat had already begun sprinkling my undertail with **salt** and **pepper**.

I had to lay it all on the line. "Fbish? Did you sbay fbish? And thbere aren't anby mbore around your **ISLAND**? Wbait, dbon't eat mbe, please— I have a grbeat idea!"

I pushed a bunch of **algae** off my snout and scurried over to Mayor Frederick Fuzzypaws, who recognized me at last. "Mr. Stilton, what are you doing here? And why are you dressed as a **SWAMP MONSTER**?"

I blushed and cut him short. "Umm . . . that story is longer than a cat's tail, but, anyway, I'm hbere to defend the pbeace!"

"Thank you, Mr. Stilton! Where have you been? We've been looking for you everywhere!" the mayor exclaimed.

I whispered, "I have an idea. **Psst . . . psssst!** What do you think, Mr. Mayor?"

I have an idea!

Umm . . .

"I think that's a great idea! Thanks, Mr. Stilton! This could help keep peace on Mouse Island!"

Then **Frederick Fuzzypaws** turned to **Bengal Longhair** and the other cats in the room. "This is our peace proposal: We will allow you to **fish** around our island, where the fish are delicious and abundant. In exchange, you will work hard not to **attack** Mouse Island. What do you say?"

Bengal Longhair licked his whiskers and rubbed his belly. "Okay, I agree. I mean, put your paw here, rat! Where is the treaty? I'll sign at once! I'm so terribly hungry! When do we eat?"

Frederick Fuzzypaws quickly handed him a scroll, and . . . **Bengal Longhair** signed it!

Our plan worked!

We saved Mouse Island!

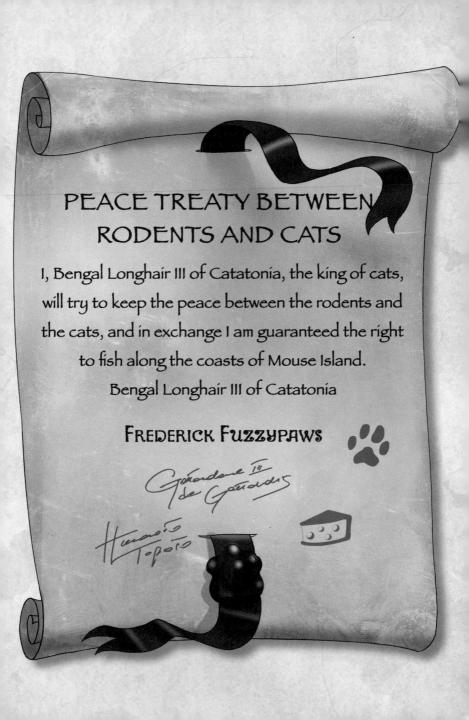

PEACE TREATY BETWEEN RODENTS AND CATS

I, Bengal Longhair III of Catatonia, the king of cats, will try to keep the peace between the rodents and the cats, and in exchange I am guaranteed the right to fish along the coasts of Mouse Island.

Bengal Longhair III of Catatonia

FREDERICK FUZZYPAWS

A few hours later, we went back to *The Rodent's Gazette*, and Bengal Longhair left for Cat Island. But first, he asked the island's best chefs to prepare him an enormouse **feast** of fresh fish!

Cheese niblets, that nasty cat's appetite was gigantic!

As I watched him devour an entire platter of COD, I couldn't help thinking about how I almost ended up in that **huge belly**! I shuddered. Squeak, I'd scraped through by a whisker!

Yum!

ENOUGH WITH THE FAINTING!

Ah, yes, I had **really, really, really** made it by a whisker! Bengal Longhair had planned to eat me as an appetizer! Just thinking about it made me **scared**: my knees buckled, my whiskers broke into a cold sweat, and my snout began to spin ...

Brrrr, how scary!

I was about to *faint* when my cousin Trap pinched my snout, yelling, "Cousin, don't even think about fainting! Tonight you need to appear on my show, no excuses! So try not to faint and don't even think of getting a stomachache, a tail-ache, or a paw-ache, understand? I want you in tip-top shape. Charming, lively, and looking spiffy, or you'll have to wash my socks for life!"

"All right, I will do my best . . ." I muttered, resigned.

"Well done, Cousin — I mean, assistant! Now pass me the notes that you took during the trip and that key to Atlantis! That way I can start preparing for tonight's episode!"

Suddenly, I realized that I had LOST all the notes and also the key to Atlantis! I was about to confess to Trap when the mayor arrived, sobbing with happiness. "Thank you so much.

You saved the city! I will have a **STATUE** built in your honor."

He blew his nose on my tie. When he finally calmed down, he said, "Here you go. I've already had a sketch prepared. Do you like it, Mr. Stilton?"

I tried to refuse. "Mr. Mayor, please, it's not necessary . . . I only did MY dUtY!"

"Don't worry, Mr. Stilton, I know that you are a very modest rodent. But this monument must

go up: it will be a **monument to peace**, and we will build it right in front of *The Rodent's Gazette,* because all of you **helped** restore peace to New Mouse City!"

I was about to consent when Trap grabbed the blueprints from my paw. "Hey, wait a minute. Where am I? You can't even scc me! Give it here. I'll handle this!"

In a flash, my cousin had adjusted the blueprints. Naturally, he'd made himself bigger and put

I'll handle this!

STILTON
MONUMENT

himself right in front. Wavering whiskers, Trap will never change!

I was about to **PROTEST** when Thea, Benjamin, Bugsy, and all my friends and colleagues at *The Rodent's Gazette* arrived. They picked me up carried me TRIUMPHANTLY through the streets of the city!

THE CELEBRATIONS LASTED SEVEN DAYS AND SEVEN NIGHTS!

IN SEARCH OF . . .
MYSTERIEEEES!

For seven days, all the rodents in New Mouse City thought of nothing but **CELEBRATING**. All the television shows (including Trap's) were suspended to broadcast the merriment. But at the end of the **seventh day**, everything went back to normal, and I continued my everyday life at *The Rodent's Gazette.*

To catch up with my writing, I stayed at **WORK** until deep into the night. Suddenly, I looked up and saw the **starry** sky outside my window . . . and began to think about our mouserific journey through time. It was truly an incredible adventure! As always, I had learned so much about the people of the **past** . . . and the **FUTURE!**

Just then the door to my office **BURST** open and my cousin Trap entered. "Cousinkins — I mean, assistant — are you ready? Are you ready to get your tail in gear? It's time to go in search of . . . **MYSTERIES!**"

Behind him were Thea, Benjamin, Bugsy, Misty, and Cheezum.

"Uncle G, we're ready. What about you?" Benjamin squeaked.

Misty pinched my snout. "Did you forget about the show? You're even more DISTRACTED than I am!"

Holey cheese, I had forgotten about the show that night!

Trap dragged me into a **TAXI**, and we headed to the Mouse TV studio. I quickly put on my dark suit and the dark glasses that Thea had brought for me.

"Gerry Berry, the whole city is going to watch tonight's show. *Aren't you excited?*" my sister asked.

"No, I'm not excited at all!" I protested. "I don't feel like talking in front of all of New Mouse City. Especially not when I'm dressed all in black like I'm going to a **funeral**!"

But Trap waved the contract and one of his

stinky socks under my nose, snickering, "Your choice, Cousin! Would you rather come on the show or wash my socks for life?"

So I took a deep breath and strode into the Mouse TV studio.

Trap pushed me into the television studio. "Cousin — I mean, assistant — get out the notes and the KEY TO ATLANTIS!"

Suddenly, I was in the spotlight, and I remembered something really important: I didn't have my notes, or the key to Atlantis! Squeak, what fear, what anxiety, what stress!

So I gathered my COURAGE and improvised! What else could I do?

I told the public the truth: It's always the best thing to do! I said that I had lost the notes and the key, but that wasn't important because I could tell them everything that I'd learned about

the **super-mysterious** city of Atlantis, the super-courageous Celts, the **very, very** mysterious Druids, and the **extra-super-mysterious** secret of Stonehenge . . .

And most of all I told them that the most important thing wasn't going in SEARCH of mysteries . . . but learning from the people of the past how to build a better future for everyone, **A FUTURE FULL OF PEACE!**

You want to know something? The show was an **ENORMOUSE SUCCESS** — after all, everyone's curious about mysteries! So I decided to write a **book** about our adventures in search of mysteries! And it's the book that you've just finished reading.

Until the next adventure, or my name isn't Stilton, Geronimo Stilton!

ANSWERS

Page 11
The glasses are hidden in the book on the crate near the armchair.

Pages 26-27
The paper is hidden behind the vase of roses near the pawchair.

Pages 54-55
There are 13 starfish.

Pages 82-83
There are 29 pages.

Pages 186-187
There are 23 goblets.

Pages 284-285
The fish is on the chair between the Cat King and Mayor Frederick Fuzzypaws.

Pages 228-229
① The chick is behind the basket, at the bottom left of the picture. ② The second chick is behind the rodent that is feeding the hens. ③The third is behind the rodent next to the cauldron.

①

②

③

Join me and my friends as
we travel through time in
these very special editions!

**THE JOURNEY
THROUGH TIME**

BACK IN TIME:
THE SECOND JOURNEY
THROUGH TIME

**THE RACE
AGAINST TIME:**
THE THIRD JOURNEY
THROUGH TIME

LOST IN TIME:
THE FOURTH JOURNEY
THROUGH TIME

**NO TIME
TO LOSE:**
THE FIFTH JOURNEY
THROUGH TIME

**THE TEST
OF TIME:**
THE SIXTH JOURNEY
THROUGH TIME

TIME WARP:
THE SEVENTH JOURNEY
THROUGH TIME

Don't miss a single fabumouse adventure!

Up Next:

Visit Geronimo in every universe!

Spacemice

Geronimo Stiltonix and his crew are out of this world!

Cavemice

Geronimo Stiltonoot, an ancient ancestor, is friends with the dinosaurs in the Stone Age!

Micekings

Geronimo Stiltonord live amongst the dragons in the ancient far north!

**Thea Stilton and the
Journey to the Lion's Den**

**Thea Stilton and the
Great Tulip Heist**

**Thea Stilton and the
Chocolate Sabotage**

**Thea Stilton and the
Missing Myth**

**Thea Stilton and the
Lost Letters**

**Thea Stilton and the
Tropical Treasure**

**Thea Stilton and the
Hollywood Hoax**

**Thea Stilton and the
Madagascar Madness**

**Thea Stilton and the
Frozen Fiasco**

**Thea Stilton and the
Venice Masquerade**

**Thea Stilton and the
Niagara Splash**

**Thea Stilton and the
Riddle of the Ruins**

**Thea Stilton and the
Phantom of the Orchestra**

**Thea Stilton and the
Black Forest Burglary**

**Thea Stilton and the
Race for the Gold**

Don't miss any of these exciting Thea Sisters adventures!

Thea Stilton and the Dragon's Code

Thea Stilton and the Mountain of Fire

Thea Stilton and the Ghost of the Shipwreck

Thea Stilton and the Secret City

Thea Stilton and the Mystery in Paris

Thea Stilton and the Cherry Blossom Adventure

Thea Stilton and the Star Castaways

Thea Stilton: Big Trouble in the Big Apple

Thea Stilton and the Ice Treasure

Thea Stilton and the Secret of the Old Castle

Thea Stilton and the Blue Scarab Hunt

Thea Stilton and the Prince's Emerald

Thea Stilton and the Mystery on the Orient Express

Thea Stilton and the Dancing Shadows

Thea Stilton and the Legend of the Fire Flowers

Thea Stilton and the Spanish Dance Mission